Maryan George is a teacher, conductor, instructor, arranger, composer, home poet, translator, hobby painter and now author, in addition to musician on trumpet, vocal and viola (strictly hobby!). She loves life, nature and diversity and is constantly cooking up new stories. Maryan wrote her first story—for the desk drawer—at the age of eight. Living in a land of sagas, ghost stories, ancient gods, fairy-tales and fantasy, it is no wonder she has ended up the way she has, living in a picture postcard with her family and four adorable cats.

To:

My man, who has loved, encouraged and supported me and put up with my antics for the last half of my life.

My children, for love, support and staunch heroism in the wake of an absentminded mother.

My sister, for being strict when I needed it and for always believing in me.

Thank you all, I love you!

Maryan George

THE FROST KING

A DRAGORA TALE

AUSTIN MACAULEY PUBLISHERS™

LONDON • CAMBRIDGE • NEW YORK • SHARJAH

A CIP catalogue record for this title is available from the British Library.

ISBN 9781528987011 (Paperback)
ISBN 9781528987028 (Hardback)
ISBN 9781528987042 (ePub e-book)
ISBN 9781528987035 (Audiobook)

www.austinmacauley.com

First Published (2021)
Austin Macauley Publishers Ltd
25 Canada Square
Canary Wharf
London
E14 5LQ

To all the great authors who have kept me company into the great unknown and led me into worlds I did not even know existed. Thank you! And to my family and my students who I in retrospect can see, have inspired some of my characters. Last, but not least, I want to give credit to my daughter, Inger Lise Hoeylo. She is quite an artist and has made the illustrations for this book, both cover and inside. Thank you dear, I am eternally grateful!

Table of Contents

Gallery of Characters

- The neighbouring or nearby countries: **Afamia, Terafuma, Orgoth, Daitemia, Nadara, Kahnie, Suder**
- **Dorth**—the largest mountain that ever was. A dormant volcano with jagged peaks, deep clefts, and an uneasy tremor in its depths
- **Elderanna**—mystery woman, sage, soothsayer, witch
- **Carina**—old and unafraid helper
- **Sashe**—queen of Terafuma
- **Amlon**—general of the Terafumian army
- **Myra Horathion**—queen of Afamia, a Gaiatlera
- **Morena**—chamber servant to Myra, deceased
- **Orsalothion**—large river in Afamia
- **Atholia**—a seer in Afamia, deceased
- **Rhanddemarr**—the sage and opponent
- **Mojastic I**—king of Arboria
- **Rajan**—general, Arborian army
- **Rhiann**—soldier in the Arborian army and gate warden
- **Ordovan**—general, Arborian Engineer Corps
- **Trecon**—general, Arborian River Corps

- **Grimor**—oldest and most revered advisor
- **Kamil**—court scribe
- **Ingan**—advisor and spellcaster
- **Tarlief**—advisor and spellcaster
- **Arcull**—recently appointed advisor, 50 years or so, grumpy and mean-looking
- **Methena**—advisor, youngest of them—a teacher
- **Joghartha**—advisor, responsible for agriculture
- **Porlene**—advisor, responsible for trade
- **Eythana**—nursemaid to prince **Myrathion I**
- **Taisha**—soldier with incredible voice

Countries & rulers:

Afamia
- Myra, 28(?)

Arboria
- Mojastic, 36

Terafuma
- Sashe, 45

Suder
- Gelroth, 37

Orgoth
- Han Sin, 57

Daitemia
- Jolanga, 48

Nadara (or Maigarr)
- Kerrsh, 57

Kahnie
- Harjarr, 47

Myra Horathion

Queen of Afamia, 28 (?)
Morena (chamber maid - deceased)
Atholia (seer—deceased)
Orsalothion (big river)
Gaiatlera (the earth fairies)

Afamia:
Grasslands, rivers, lakes, second most important

Arboria:
Woodland, large forests, rivers and lakes; focus in story, hilly country

Terafuma:
Volcanic activity, unrestful landscape, 64 active volcanoes—"fire hills"

Suder: desert
Hot, sandy and arid landscape, sparsely populated, most are trekkers

Orgoth:
Orientally inspired, very macho, slavery, marsh and turf, horseland

Daitemia: female warriors
Female dominion, quiet, sandy landscapes, universities

Nadara: Maigarr—above ground, Dorthnonder—below ground
Barren, desolate, uninhabited—at least above ground, birds and ghouls

Kahnie: combination Inuit/Viking
Icy land to the extreme south, glaciers, polar warriors

The world: Dragora	Sashe: - Queen of Terafuma - Amlon; general

Elderanna—the wise and powerful:

- Wise woman, witch, soothsayer, fortune teller, strong defender—no age
- Has a blurred past that comes clearer as the story progresses
- Carina (old, but unafraid)

Mojastic I:

- King of Arboria—36
- Myrathion I son of Myra and
- Three generals: Mojastic I
- Rajan—44
- Ordovan—56
- Trecon—52
- Seven advisors:
- Grimor—70
- Ingan—32
- Tarlief—24
- Arcull—50
- Methena—21
- Joghartha—27
- Porlene—33

Rhanddemarr - the Sage

- o Sorcerer, villain, opponent, harsh, hard, cold, but mighty, age old, unchanging
- o Kerrsh, king of Nadara (or Maigarr)
- o Maigarrians—inhabitants of Dorthnonder (the land under Dorth)
- o According to myth, the peoples of Nadara once lived on the surface—in Maigarr—but were forced underground by a natural disaster long, long ago

Organisation of the Arborian army:

Combat Group > 5 soldiers

Unit > 5 combat groups > 25 strong

Division > 4 Units > 100 strong

Chamber > 5 Divisions > 500 strong

Regular army: 4 Chambers—each led by a general lieutenant > General Rajan

(Navy or) River Corps > 1 Unit > General Trecon

Engineer Corps > 1 Unit > General Ordovan

Officers: Theyn, Argil, and Benach

Soldiers mentioned by name: Rhiann, Taisha

Magical capabilities:

Spellcasting

Cursing

Foretelling

Sinestral > scouting

Elaidar—"bird of prey: hovering, soaring, scouting, and invisible"

Clairvoyance—foreseeing the future

Shifting—teleportation

Inhabitants of Dorthnonder

- ➤ **Drenklich**—flying snake with eagle wings and troll's head
- ➤ **Daemoin**—snake-shaped creatures with venom and constrictor abilities, immune to poison and exceptionally strong.

- ➤ **Greitsch**—lizard-like creature, with serpent head and row upon row of sharp teeth.
- ➤ **Noctemar**—a being of darkness that leeches the memories, life force, and soul out of the creatures it attacks. Prefers large prey—humans, for example.
- ➤ **Ghalorr**—a fire-horse: flaming being in horse's shape that can fly without wings. Light up the night sky like comets and are often mistaken for these until they come up close.
- ➤ **Chaiga**—small, furry creatures that will completely bewilder anyone that tries to stare at them for long, due to their speed. Essentially harmless but can bite when alarmed.
- ➤ <u>**Illiot**</u>—one of the chiefs of the Chaigas.
- ➤ **Boreala**—white dragon: benevolent creature from ancient mythology, said to be Ahroree's steed of choice
- ➤ **"Giant centipede"**—grotesquely altered and enlarged insect, voracious and dangerous
- ➤ **Plants, animals, natural sites/formations:**
- ➤ **Bahliama trees**—tall trees with dense foliage, solid dark grey trunks, six-tongued leaves—dark green over and purple under, and intensely blue flowers all through the summer.
- ➤ **Arrca**—large river that runs past the town/village of Arboria.
- ➤ **Eyadia**—the mountain range that runs along the border between Mount Dorth and the countries to the south (Afamia, Arboria)

Prologue: The Hidden and Forgotten

"You!" the voice was stern and fraught with anger. "I curse you for what you have done! You midget, you witch, you traitor!" Choking on his words, spitting them out like pieces of coal, glowing red. Then—his voice changed—and for the first time she felt a pang of fear. He raised his hands to the level of his shoulders, while he chanted in an ancient tongue.

"I curse you to oblivion, to humanity, to solitude, to silence! In their shape you will see the fruits of your labour go to waste. As one of them, you will feel mortality weigh you down, while your memory flies on the wild winds." As his words took hold, she felt herself slipping, her body and mind parting ways; she screamed in agony and fear.

He ended, sneering at her, "Only a lover can wake you from this, and I am the one you loved!" Laughing wildly, he then shoved her over the cliff's edge and watched her plunge into darkness...

In the world of the elder days, the landscape looked very different from now. Mountains were taller, more imposing, rivers were wilder or wider, brooks were livelier, winds were stronger, in other words, there was a lot more of everything— a 'moreness' if you will. More weather, more animals, more life—it was an abundancy of all things that sometimes could make a person gasp for air.

In this world women and men could live joyfully with the seasons slowly changing around them. But—of course—if the good things were so pronounced, then the dark, terrible things that existed were also more, and stronger.

A world so joyous could easily forget that which lay just beyond—or below—the vision of its inhabitants, and that was precisely what had happened. For in its deeps, in the huge, dark caverns of the mountains that stretched for miles without end into the earth, there lived…other beings. Beings that never saw the light, that never breathed the fresh air, and that existed without any purpose of entering the day above. These two worlds—for they were two distinct worlds—never crossed each other's paths, never knew of the existence of each other, and certainly no one ever planned for them to do so. And so it went on forever—or could have.

But one terribly chilling night—when the ground froze solid underneath the North Star and the skies were so clear you could see eternity—everything changed.

----- " ----- " ----- " ----- " ----- " ----- " ----- " -----

First, there was only white mist—like cotton, only much, much softer and ethereal—swimming around her like eddies in a stream, bobbing and creating waves that disappeared just as fast as they appeared. Then the fog solidified, or rather, you got the impression that there was something in the fog— something big. This would seem impossible, knowing that she was floating around at a staggering height, but still that feeling persisted—the feeling of eeriness and, for lack of a better word, solidity. As she sailed through the clouds, she began to see the contours of something immense in front of, and a little below, her vantage point. This immense structure or thing sailed slowly towards her, like a bank appearing slowly out of the sea, or a treasure hidden in the sand, suddenly exposed by the wind.

And then, at once, it was there! As she dipped out of the upper cloud cover, there materialised before her the upper jagged peaks of a mountain so huge it was almost unfathomable. Wild, pointed rocks seemed to jab at her as she drifted past them, hostile and barren as only high-mountain areas can seem. Below her she could vaguely see the mountain continuing down and getting lost in the clouds once again. She was aware that on either side of her, peaks were punching holes in the clouds hiding the ground from sight while deep crevasses gave the impression of the mountain tearing itself apart with brute strength.

A wind was rising in the east—rising with the dawn—and building to a gale that drove the clouds westward, exposing the mountain in all its terrifying glory. She could see now that what she had mistaken for the top of the mountain, in reality, was the peak of the eastern spur. The main top of the mountain lay almost exactly in the middle and was so tall that it was lost in the perpetual twilight of the upper atmosphere. The body of the mountain spread in all directions and covered the whole horizon from where she was. It was quite simply so immense; it defied all description. She continued her descent slowly, with the wind softly whispering all around her—or was it the wind? The sound was eerie and at the same time low-pitched, like the voice of a man, but without words that *she could recognise. It was too faint, however, to make out for certain.*

As she neared the base of this monster, she glanced up to see how it looked from here, and the only word she found in her mind, was 'forbidding'—the mountain was one big, horrendous omen, an enormous shadow in the future of this world. Then she looked down, heavyhearted and sad, and by her feet she saw a little white flower. A tear fell from her eyes and watered the tiny life in the desolate landscape and all the while she thought, "There is still hope, even when all seems lost, but we may have to lose everything to find it…" The faint sound of wind suddenly became louder, roaring with the voices of strange beasts, and a voice wormed its way out of the cacophony; a cold and harsh sound it was, filled with menace, and yet majestic in a strange way. It was…singing? No! It was chanting, and its words were more than she could bear as it spoke of the return to oblivion and the ban of light. A shadow suddenly blocked out the pale light and cast everything into darkness while a freezing cold ate its way into her body, and on the heels of that came the voice, "I will find you!" Elderanna screamed her way into waking.

What really got to her, was that she could never remember what she had dreamed. It was one misty, foggy haze, filled with dreary, but vague shapes and a feeling of utter horror— a terror so bad it froze her bones and made her mind go blank, even in the middle of summer. As time went by, the memory faded, but still she would get that feeling of terror every time she thought about it. It scared her, terrified her, terrorised her—more than anything; object, animal or human ever could. Time went by and still it faded, but never quite away—

it always remained at the threshold of her mind with the unanswered questions, "Who are you? Who am I? What do you want from me???"

Chapter 1
Beginnings and Endings

The queen was dreaming. She was being chased by something she had never seen, something she could not name, something that terrified her so badly it almost made her heart stop. Her feet were pounding against the stony ground, bruising her soles and cutting her toes. Her hair was getting caught in branches and twigs that threatened to rip it off her head, and all the while she could hear her attacker—not human, of that she was certain—behind her, coming ever nearer, despite everything she tried. In the quiet of her surroundings, the sound of her moans and thrashings were very loud. A shadow appeared in the doorway to her room, her lady-in-waiting, Morena, with a very anxious look on her face. "My lady, wake up!" But she did not—she could not. Tied in the dream she was lost in a land of shadows, whispers and mist—the most terrifying she had ever experienced—and she could not find her way out, nor did she know how she got there in the first place. An earth-shattering, loud bang suddenly broke and hammered into her skull. She woke screaming...

If you came flying through the air over the northern end of the continent and dove through the clouds, you would be looking down on a sea of green. On closer inspection, you would realise that you were looking at great, rolling hills, covered in trees. Numerous hues and shades of green would explode towards you as you descended, and individual trees would become visible: old, new, straight, twisted and crooked, knotted, stunted and tall. Some of the trees, many in fact, were giants, stretching towards the sky like towers.

Between the trees you would see rivers, wide, slow and majestic, following the terrain in the bottom of the valleys, as well as torrential and cascading waterfalls tumbling down the steep sides of the hills. Glades would be visible as you came nearer, together with orchards and fields, hamlets and villages, and in the centre of the rolling landscape, lay a small town with a castle situated behind it. This was the kingdom of Arboria.

It was a small kingdom as far as inhabitants go, but prosperous for its size. There was no hunger, everyone had enough to eat, good, warm clothes for winter and cool garments for summer. The houses were not tall; one or two-storey houses in which they lived and had their small businesses or shops. Now, with the distances to neighbouring countries being quite large, they did not have a lot of trade from abroad or send off lots of goods in trade on a daily basis. Most of their trade was of the internal kind, but it was enough to keep the shopkeepers, businesses and traders busy. Children were well cared for, all of them went to school, and there were very few children's diseases to make them ill. And, of course, if they were taken ill, then the village wise woman was more than capable of nursing them back to health again.

This wise woman, or witch, as they would call her who ended up on the wrong side of her, was almost as ancient as the oak trees that surrounded her little cabin. Set apart from the rest of the village, up a hill and about a hundred strides into a grove on the outskirts of the forest, her cabin was an island of calm in the everyday hustle and bustle of village life. Her name was Elderanna, and she had been the kingdom's sage, healer and soothsayer for longer than anyone could remember. Old she was, and yet not, for her countenance was free of any of the signs that usually accompany old age: wrinkles, saggy skin and blotches. None of those were visible or even present; her skin was like the skin of a new-born babe—soft, smooth and beautifully even. Her body was strong and supple, her limbs—though she was small in stature—strong and lithe. The only outward sign of her age— visible at first sight—was her hair: stunning, long, lush and snowy-white, almost silver. When you got closer, however, and looked into her deep, dark eyes, you found yourself in a well of knowledge and history that stretched seemingly forever into the depths. You could drown in those eyes, and there were few who could endure her gaze for long.

Yes, she was indeed ancient, but still she was beautiful. Beautiful like a river can be—gorgeous in fact—and although she was older than any of the people in the town of Arboria liked to think of or could imagine, still she was young; ancient, but hale, like a force of nature that never grows old and frail, only wise and tough. Even the king, the revered Mojastic the first, depended upon her to foresee the immediate future and so make provisions for weather, crops, epidemics and other preventable mishaps. Not that there had been many of those, but he still found security in her presence.

Mojastic the first was, as the name suggests, the first in his line to wear this name, but he did not let that weigh him down. He came from a long line of chieftains that had only five generations ago, become kings. Marych had been the first king of his line, then they had had Moroch the first and the second, and then Mydrych, who was Mojastic's father. All of them had been good kings if not great, and Mojastic was determined that he was not going to bring shame over their memory. He was a well-built man: tall and broad-shouldered, with long, dark auburn hair usually kept in a ponytail. His eyes were bluish-grey, and he had a mouth that was prone to laughter and which always had a smile hidden in his beard. But he needed a wife, a queen, to continue the family line, secure peace and bring prosperity to his kingdom. Not much to ask for in a wife, you might say, but good candidates were hard to come by and time was not on his side. Albeit still young, only 36, and looking forward to a long and healthy life as his forebears had had, the question of a wife still gnawed on his mind.

Lately, however, something more was beginning to worry him, or bother him. He had begun having this really weird feeling or notion. It was like an uneasiness of the mind, or a sinking feeling in his gut; an almost undetectable quirk, but a real one, nonetheless. Also, he had begun having nightmares or visions in his dreams. Well, he had a feeling it had actually started a long, long time ago, but it was only recently—in the past few years—that he had slowly started to become aware of it. And now it was becoming stronger, more intense, or he was becoming more sensitised; he was not sure which. One thing was certain, though, things were speeding up, gathering pace, and Arboria was right in the middle of events that were unfurling, like a tuft of grass in the middle of a field with the banners of an army in the distance, completely surrounding it.

Or was that the right image? He did not know. One thing he had not done, he had not discussed this with anyone yet—neither his advisors nor his generals had been notified of the unease that was beleaguering him, but they would have to be—sooner rather than later—for he could sense that something was going to happen, the only questions were: When and What?

Since he had not discussed this with anyone, he had no way of knowing if others were experiencing the same or similar sensations, but—unknown to him—events were unfolding that would rapidly force the question to be asked.

Then one day, one of the first days of spring, someone appeared in the most surprising manner: a resourceful, smart and yes, beautiful, young woman turned quite unexpectedly up in the village. Or she snuck into the village you might say, because no one saw her enter it by any of the usual paths or tracks. She might just as well have been dropped there by an eagle, if such had been possible, but, for all the people of Arboria knew, it was not. Her appearance was magical, nonetheless. The name she gave when asked was Myra Horathion, and she asked to be taken to the king for she had a message of importance for his ears only. Being young and beautiful, as before mentioned, she had no scarcity of volunteers and could take her pick of guide.

At the castle, she was escorted up into the king's private study to deliver her message and they were closeted in there for quite a long time, so long in fact, that the guards standing by the door were beginning to get slightly apprehensive. But then the door opened and the king stepped outside to give orders to his soldiers and advisors that were also standing by. This was odd to begin with, because any orders the king had hitherto spoken had been in the form of requests, not barked-out orders as such. It made them all the more curious and slightly nervous, but they did not get any explanation yet. Elderanna was in her garden at the back of her little cottage—at least it seemed small from the outside—tending the little saplings: roses, lilies, forget-me-nots, and many other plants and flowers, some of them completely unknown to the people—a select few—who were allowed into that garden. Most were grown for medical purposes, but some were only grown for their beauty, the roses were in this category. This year it looked as if they were going to be stunning, already showing plump little knots on their branches, and flaunting a lush, deep green mass of leaves. Granted, there were not many who had set foot in her garden, it was hedged in by hawthorns. Only Mojastic and a handful of wise women from the neighbouring villages had had that honour; she kept her garden private, on account of many of the plants being poisonous. When the messenger from the king arrived, he was prepared to raise his voice in front of the cottage to alert her of his presence, but this proved unnecessary. She was coming around the corner as he opened his mouth to shout and his call died in his throat. Somehow, she knew—she always knew. She nodded at him and stepped quickly into the wagon waiting to bring them back to the castle promptly. The king's orders were swiftly complied with and the people who had been called for quickly gathered in a large, but somewhat unused room, the council chamber, where the war council were supposed to gather in times of crisis, not that it ever had, until now that was.

The council chamber was austere and almost naked. It was furbished only with what was necessary: a large table, oval in shape, and chairs, lamps that lit the room with a stark glow, and maps of Arboria and the surrounding kingdoms—both topographic and demographic. In this room, they now assembled: the king, of course, Myra, Elderanna, the advisors—there were seven of those, Grimor, Arcull, Ingan, Tarlief, Methena, Joghartha and Porlene, the king's generals—three in all; Rajan, Ordovan, and Trecon—and a scribe, namely Kamil the court scribe, to keep record of their deliberations. As they sat down to begin, many curious glances were directed toward Myra, but no questions were asked as yet. Myra on her part was calm and pensive, lost in her own thoughts as it seemed, but this did not prevent her casting some glances of her own, most of them in the direction of Elderanna.

The king stood up, his eyes surveyed the room and took in all their faces, so eager and anxious, before he finally spoke. His words hit them with the force of an earthquake or a sudden stroke of lightning, "We are at war!"

The only sound in the night was the sound of her sobbing. Morena stood helplessly by all the while trying to console her, but without knowing what to say. She had sent for the soothsayer as well as the healer, and included two of the advisors, but Morena still wished she could do more. At last, the queen's sobs slowed to a standstill, and she raised her head. "Are the stars out?" she asked. Morena—baffled by the question—answered her affirmatively. The queen went to the window—slowly, as if it hurt her to walk—and gazed out at the sky. Strewn out above her head were thousands upon thousands of stars, twinkling in the night sky like diamonds.

Everything—the whole world—was quiet and at perfect rest.
Everything, that was, except her mind.

Chapter 2
Myra's Tale

The room, which until then had been filled with curious babbling, whispering, and questions, fell abruptly quiet. It was as if someone had taken a pair of scissors and just cut the sound. In the ensuing silence, the faint notes of birdsong which came in through the vents, were as loud as thunder. Finally, one old and revered advisor—Grimor, the oldest and most venerable of them all, asked in a cracking and quavering voice, clearly rattled, "Excuse me, Sir, but did you say…war?"

"Yes," the king replied, looking grave and sad. From being good-humoured and jolly this morning, his countenance was now plagued with concern and worry, etching fine lines between his brows. At the same time, there was an air of stunnedness about him, as if he himself did not quite believe what he had just said. That same air was evident on the faces of all the people in the room, except for Myra's. Hers was a face with determination written in every beautiful line. Her eyes, fascinating with their hues of grey, blue or green—depending on her mood—were now steely grey and hard, if that was a word one could use about such a lovely lady. But there could be no doubt she was there for a grave cause and that she meant business.

Mojastic beckoned her forward, and she slid gracefully and effortlessly to the foreground. Standing in front of everyone, she bowed slightly and then curtseyed to them. This was the first opportunity they had for studying her, and study they did. Every eye in the room was fixed on her and drank in all the details of her appearance; from the blonde-red hair, glowing and flowing down her back in unruly curls, to her tall, slender, but full-bodied figure. They took in her finely chiselled face and her beautiful complexion; golden-brown and sun-kissed. But it was her eyes that held them; large, slightly slanted, and—for the moment—dark grey in colour, soft, and at the same time, brilliant. Every person in the room felt warmed by those eyes when they rested on them for a moment. They all acknowledged her by bowing their heads to her and then Mojastic said, "This is Myra Horathion. She has come a long way to give me terrifying news and to ask my involvement in a situation which has become increasingly dangerous. But she will tell you the story in her own words." And then the tale of Myra commenced.

"Thank you, sire," she said, and continued, "I come from the land of the river dragons and the talking birds, Afamia, beyond the mountains of Nod to the east of Arboria. We, who live there, have known nothing but peace for ages and our land has hitherto been untroubled by any of the calamities that strike from time to time. The water has flowed gently down the rivers, or torrentially in the waterfalls, our forests have been lush and green, our flatlands fertile and abounding with wildlife, and the snows on our mountaintops have been eternal and quiet in contemplation of the ages. But that has all changed. The winds have started to blow from the north, cold and wet, and the snow no longer stays on the mountaintops. It frequently covers the ground in drifts together with a sheet of ice and sleet. The harvest has failed three years in a row, our wildlife and game are disappearing, our forests are turning damp and soggy, and with the falling temperatures the rivers alternate between freezing and overflowing. In short, life is difficult right now. But if it were only these calamities that assailed us, we could handle them ourselves. It seems, however, that a deeper purpose is revealed, and not a good one. A sinister mind is behind it all, controlling the forces of nature and twisting them to its own ends, forcing us into a position of fight or flight and tormenting us in order to secure our surrender. The most devastating thought of them all is that we knew this was coming. All of this is as was foretold of old, in the Prophecy of the Frost King."

The stunned silence that ensued was only broken when a deep voice said quietly, "Who is behind this, did you say?"

"I have not named him, yet, for his name is an abhorrence to my people, but I will!" said Myra, in response. The deep voice belonged to a woman, the one of four in the chamber besides Myra, and had a vigour and strength far younger than her years. Elderanna had spoken up and left the rest of the congregation silent and subdued. Myra smiled at her with an almost knowing look in her eyes and Elderanna looked back, straight as a line.

Once again Elderanna spoke, "Will you not name him now, the adversary of olden ages? He, whose stirrings are like the omen of doom?"

Myra looked down for a second, as if to collect herself. And then, lifting her face and looking straight into their eyes as she looked around, she spoke again, "He is old, older than our time reckoning, and he is strong, stronger than I like to think of. His powers are both subtle, as he directs things by the push and pull of his will and orders them to behave the way he wants them to, and they are direct, as he can do terrible but awesome things with his spells. He thinks of himself as 'The Firstborn Ruler' and his ambition is to order all things to his liking. I said, he has been plaguing us with bad weather and shifts in the seasons, but that is only the tip of the iceberg. From old, gathering his strength from darkness, he was in opposition to light and day, and this led to a bitter fight with The Lady of Light. He fought long and hard to destroy her or minimise her power, destroying the lands and laying wide areas waste with his spells. But he fought in vain, and daylight has been our constant companion ever since. However, he has neither given up the fight nor his purpose. He has only been resting, re-charging himself, and now he deems the time ripe and his strength sufficient to take up the fight again. His name is…" She hesitated, then she pushed on, "His name is Rhanddemarr—The Sage—but we seldom name him, for to name a foe is to us to concede that foe power, and this we are loath to do."

As she paused her narrative, a choir of questions, exclamations and general confusion broke loose, and Mojastic was forced to pound the table to restore order to the congregation. When finally, the room was quiet once again, General Rajan, who commanded what forces they had in Arboria, got permission to speak.

"Lady," he began, "we would like to know some more about your people, your country and most of all: how you can be sure that this sorcerer is behind your calamities? Also, what is this prophecy you are talking about?"

"General...Rajan?" she replied, "As your questions call for a rather thorough and therefore lengthy answer, I would like to sit down. I have had a hard journey getting here and my feet are faltering."

An upholstered chair was procured for her, and she began her narrative in earnest, "Many ages ago, when the world was young and the air was full of promise, my people awakened by the banks of the river Orsalothion. Yes," she said, directing her gaze at Elderanna, "you guessed rightly. I am of the Gaiatlera, as we call ourselves. You have another name for us I have heard?"

Elderanna nodded, "We call you Earth-fairies," she said.

"Earth-fairies," said Myra, smiling to herself, "that sounds nice, and a little bit disbelieving perhaps. But be that as it may, we lived quietly and joyfully by the river, enjoying life and all its gifts, carefully studying the world and its inhabitants while being a part of it all. I remember seeing the stars reflected in the water like strands of pearls, or the Winter-Road of the sky shining softly in the pond." She paused for a moment, lost in thought, but then took up the thread of her story again. "As the years rolled by, becoming millennia, we noticed a subtle change in the world, but we could not yet detect the source, nor pinpoint exactly what was off. It was more a feeling, like perhaps a forgotten bad dream, than anything solid, but our lives were plagued by this gnawing unrest. Then the seer, Atholia, had a vision. What she saw, frightened her so much that it left her speechless for over a year. After that year, in which she rapidly declined, she only spoke once, then waned away. In more brutal terms, she

34

died, the first, and at that point in time, only one of our people to ever do that. We were completely overcome with our loss and stunned by it, because we had never met with anything like it and did not know where to turn for solace. The words which she spoke, her last message to us, has since been on the minds of every one of our people, and we keep it always in our hearts. They are known as 'The Prophecy of the Frost King'.

Then Myra took a breath and sipped some water from a goblet set before her, before continuing. The council sat there, completely still, all ears, their eyes fixated on her face.

"The Prophecy has been recorded and put down in writing in our Hall of Remembrance and is also to be found on the wall of our council chamber where counsels are taken, and advice sometimes given. It guides every move and colours every policy we make. But it was also spoken here in the kingdom of Arboria of old. I feel certain that some record of it must be kept somewhere?" She looked around inquiringly. The council sat there, flabbergasted, just looking from one to the other. That is, all but one of them: Elderanna sighed and stood up. In spite of her small and slender body, she still made her presence known and her authority felt through her stance.

"I sincerely hoped this day would not come while I existed," she began, looking sad and worried at the same time. "The Prophecy is known to only a select few who all have sworn to keep it safe, to remember it, and to pass it on in time to the people chosen for this task. In our kingdom, it has always been in the possession of the village Sage, in other words, the village wise woman. It has been kept a secret even from before the time of the kings, when this was just a wilder land with scattered little hamlets in the woods."

Now, with the attention of the whole council upon her, she sighed again and went on, "The Prophecy runs as follows…" Here she straightened herself up, her voice became commanding, somehow stern, and very clear, while her face seemed to be lit from within.

"In the years when the North wind is blowing,
When the game and the fruits grow scarce.
When the farmer won't reap what he's sowing,
And the livestock will wither from fears.

"When the lands are plunged into darkness,
And the stars are erased from the sky.
When the rivers to ice are all frozen,
And the birds from the woodlands do fly.

"With the howling of sorrowful wolves
And the crying of hungering babes.
With the stillborn and wasting calves
And foundering fish under waves.

"Then the lands will be crowded with daimons,
And the screaming of ravenous ghouls.
As they lust for despair and for terror,
And they laugh as we fear for our souls.

"Now the king will arise from the ashes
That smoulders and burns in his eyes.
The forgotten and lonely that washes
All the pains of this world aside.

"He will conquer the Sage and give welcome
to an era of light and bloom
If he can persist in his struggle.
If not, we all go to our doom."

Completing the speaking of the prophecy, she dropped to her chair again, exhausted. It was as if the act of breaking a centuries old silence had drained her of all her energy. But it only lasted a moment, and then she lifted her eyes to them and looked intently at each and every person in the council chamber. The king cleared his throat, "Well, that was a bit of a surprise. Who could have known that even in our kingdom such secrets were being kept?" His words acted as a catalyst or the breaking of a dam; everyone spoke at the same time yet again, and this time it was a note of nervousness and haste in their voices.

"What shall we do?"

"How do we know that these are the times mentioned in the prophecy?"

"What do our neighbours do or say about this?"

"How will the military avail us if there is no tangible enemy to defend against?"

"Can we trust these tidings, or are they presented to us with a purpose of misleading us?"

"QUIET!" thundered the king, sending everyone reeling, including Myra and Elderanna this time. None of those present, had ever heard him raise his voice to anyone or for anything, so the shock of him doing so was enough to make some of them faint. As they slowly got their bearings, he spoke again, calmly this time, "Now is not the time for panic. Rhanddemarr is an unknown adversary to us, but his malevolence has long haunted these lands with dark thoughts and worries that lie just beyond the tip of your tongue or in the very back of your mind. You know that there is something there, but you cannot say what it is or whence it comes. There are groves in the woods that of old have been peaceful and calm places, oases for contemplation and quiet thought. These have changed or have been changed. What used to be groves are now swamps, and if you go there you are sure to get lost or worse."

He surveyed the faces in the ring, looking for disagreement, but found none. Continuing in the same, calm tone he advised them to keep still, calm and collected. He then spoke to the servants waiting outside the door, ordering food to be prepared and served, drinks and refreshments to be made available in the chamber, in addition to more comfortable chairs for everyone present. As he explained to the servants, they were going to be secluded in the chamber for quite a while and needed their strength and wits about them. Then he addressed the council again, "Take what refreshment you feel is needed. Get some air, stretch your legs and freshen up. When we sit down again, we will not leave this room until we have a clear strategy and plan for the upcoming months, or years if needed. We have got to prepare for war, and heavy though this burden may be, it would be heavier if we buried our faces in the tall grass and pretended that everything was good, only to wake up in the face of emergency and crisis and with no plan for how to deal with it. Or worse, suddenly find ourselves face to face with an enemy of which we knew nothing." Silently, the council got to their feet, but as they neared the door and some of them were about to step outside, he said with a stern voice, "And remember, nothing you have heard in this room, can be discussed with anyone outside these walls, at least not yet!" They looked at each other, and then nodded in consent as they left.

The huddled figures that made their way to the queen's chambers were quiet and wearing troubled expressions. They entered her rooms hurriedly, greeted each other and sat down around the table in the outer chamber. The healer appeared in the doorway, looked at them shortly and then retreated into the bedchamber. After a few moments, the queen made her entry. She looked composed, but harrowed and tired, and she had an expression on her face that neither of the group had ever seen before—a mingled look of desperation and determination. She looked at each of them in turn before greeting them with the words, "The end of our world is here."

Chapter 3
The War Council

An hour later, they re-assembled in the council chamber. The chamber itself had been altered since they last saw it. More maps had been hung on the walls, these covering the lands further afield: Afamia, Terafuma, Orgoth, Daitemia, and of course the mountain of Dorth and Nadara. Even Kahnie, the cold and windy land to the south, and Suder, with its burning deserts, were represented in the array that was hung around the room. A bigger table had been set in the middle of the floor, one which was equipped with a model of the surrounding lands; mountains, rivers, fields and woods, all clearly depicted in miniature. The council chamber seemed darker, somehow, and more sinister than it had been on their previous meeting. Of course, the time of day might have something to do with it, but the main reason was to be found in their attitude and what was weighing on their minds when they entered.

With everybody present and seated, the king called the council opened and their deliberations began in earnest. A council meeting can be long and tedious work, and this was made even longer by the fact that the whole situation felt awkward and strange to all but a few of them. It was to the mountain of Dorth that they first turned their attention, since it was, after all, their nearest neighbour. Standing alone, a short distance beyond the end of the Jotnesal Range's northernmost point, it was a huge mass of stone, grey and cold. It was so wide that it covered the whole horizon and rose to an almost unbelievable height. 28000 metres, or 61600 feet, it rose into the sky. The mountain of Dorth was in fact an old volcano that had been active in the days of the Awakening, but which had long since been quiet and was thought to be extinct. The summit was always hidden in the eternal twilight of the upper atmosphere, and the sides of its many peaks were slippery and wet when it was raining, frosted and deadly when it was snowing. It was a depressing enough thing to think about even without a malicious sorcerer hiding inside it. Beyond Dorth there were the wastelands that they called Nadara, all desolate and empty. Or so they believed, anyway. It was hard to be sure of anything when the land was situated so far away and the journey to get there was first a trail through the thick forests of Arboria, most of them unmapped and pathless, and then the journey continued further on trails full of treacherous pits, gaping fissures and dangers unknown. It was a hard journey at best and one that they did not cherish the thought of making. In fact, not one of them looked forward to such an adventure, if adventure was the right word!

As the hours passed, the council continued its deliberations. Sometimes a voice could be heard rising over the rest, at other times there would be no sound at all, only the whispering sound of pages being turned, or maps being shifted. The council had a lot of reading to do, to catch up on their knowledge of the surrounding countries. Mojastic was sitting still, staring into the air. He was pensive, almost brooding, and did not yet participate in the discussions that took place around him. Still, he did not seem anonymous or displaced. He seemed even more the centre of the room, the more he withdrew himself from it. Everyone was all the time sending glances in his direction, asking approval for their ideas with their eyes, or looking at him questioningly whenever they were in doubt about what to look at or which option to choose. In all their deliberations, their attention turned constantly to Mojastic.

Myra and Elderanna found themselves next to each other, in front of the maps. They looked silently into each other's eyes, then they smiled for the first time that day. "So, a daughter of the River people—the Gaiatlera—has come to grace our land," said Elderanna, her voice without any trace of scorn or mockery.

Myra nodded, suddenly shy, "Yes. I've come here to forge a union, or a consolidation, for the difficult times that lie ahead. But I'm uncertain about how to proceed, the…people of Arboria seem to need many words before they go into action?"

Elderanna smiled. A slow smile that lit up her face and transformed it into something completely new, yet at the same time ancient and beautiful, like a work of art.

"You almost said humans," she remarked. Laughing a little and blushing, Myra replied, "Yes, I almost did. But you must remember, these people are new to me, though I find them endearing, in their own way. And some of them more than others, I might also say."

With this, she looked straight at Mojastic. Elderanna, following her gaze, chuckled, "We have an excellent king, don't we?"

Now, Myra was blushing in earnest. With a somewhat strange smile she whispered, "Yes, indeed you do, and that makes the task ahead of me easier and harder at the same time."

Elderanna looked at her questioningly, "What do you mean your highness?" Startled, Myra looked at her, suddenly wide-eyed.

"You didn't think you could hide your lineage from me for long, did you?" said Elderanna, a knowing smile lingering about her lips.

Myra looked down, then she raised her gaze to Elderanna's face, "No, I might have guessed that there was more to you than 'just' a village wise woman. You have the air of the Gaiatlera about you, but how did you come to be here in the first place?"

Elderanna smiled thoughtfully, then she spoke, "I remember—from far down in my memory—being a young lass like you, jumping around from one thing to another, smelling every flower, tasting the fruits of the earth, enjoying life to its fullest. Yet something was always a little off track, or key, if you will. Like a sweet, but dissonant tone, far off in the distance, almost out of range. I recall hearing the whispering of voices, voices that sounded as if they were in my head. This was not the case though, as I found out soon enough. The voices were real. They were the voices of the nature around me, voices of the trees, the rivers, the birds, the dragons, even the sky. These voices spoke to me in whispered tones, and what they had to tell me was terrifying. They spoke of a darkness somewhere, sometime in the future, a war to be fought, and a foe to be vanquished, once and for all, if that was at all possible." She paused, drinking some wine from a flagon, and continued. All the while Myra was sitting listening, hanging on every word. "In the end, I had to sit down and listen to them for real and ask questions. One thing was what they were telling me, another was, Why me? And then there were the questions that came in the wake of these, like, who do you expect me to tell it to? What do you want from me? And finally, what fate is lying before me? I was shocked, bewildered and completely at a loss, and so I went to see the only person that I thought could help me. She was a kind, caring and fundamentally unafraid woman by the name of Carina. She told me to spend my time alone, in the manner of ancient tribes, for an unspecified duration, until the voices became clear to me and I could hear their message without interference from the world. So, I went up in the mountain and sat there on a secluded shelf in the mountainside.

"The bustle of the world ground slowly to a halt. The noises of wind and birds, and the creatures of the land, became faint and subdued. All around me, it seemed that the world was holding its breath. Time became something fleeting; sometimes running, sometimes stopping, sometimes dancing around, or going backwards even! And then, I could hear them clearly for the first time in my life—no longer whispers and hints, but clear and unequivocal."

Myra looked at her with respect in her eyes, "And they told you that this storm was coming and that it would be a struggle from which there could be no certainties as to the outcome." It wasn't a question—she stated it as she would state that the sky is blue when the sun shines. Elderanna smiled—a sad and wistful smile—and spoke, "Yes. They were also very clear on what they expected of me, and when

I listened to them, I found myself wishing that I could somehow have ignored them in the first place. They told me to go away from the lands I knew, and settle here in these wooded hills, to be a village wise woman and a counsellor to its people. I was also told that the wait for this struggle would be laced with increasing unrest and that people would find themselves scared seemingly for no reason whatsoever. This unrest would eventually deepen into anxiety and fear, even horror, and it would all appear to be without any hold on reality. Until the coming of the messenger from the land of the river-dragons, that was. So, you see, the coming of you into this village—this land—was the footsteps of doom, soft and sure and menacing. Who could have thought that the end of everything we know would travel in the guise of such a fair—even beautiful—lady?" This last sentence was spoken very softly, as if it was only meant for them.

Mojastic was calling the council to attention, "Everyone, please listen up. We have looked at the maps, trying to pinpoint the exact source from which this feeling emanates. And I think we have found it." He pointed to the map where they could see Arboria and the region to the north. "From the accounts that we have heard, the feeling of unrest, of bad dreams and nightmares, first entered our kingdom from the direction of the mountain of Dorth. Then it gradually spread like water in a pool until it covered the whole kingdom, and still more waves kept coming, growing stronger all the time. But always discreet, always so quiet that it could be just our imaginations. If it had not affected everyone, that is." He stopped and looked at them, surprisingly enough with a wry smile on his face, "This is not the enemy we have prepared for, is it? Yet, we will have to do something about the situation."

"Our first priority should be to counter these attacks by putting spells over the population to shield them from the force of the dreams. Then we are going to have to communicate with the kingdoms to the south and east of us, to hear if they are experiencing something similar to what we and the Gaiatlera are. We will also have to take common counsel for the situation and coordinate our efforts to fight back and at the same time shield our kingdoms from his powers, if that is at all possible. I fear that this unrest we are feeling is only the beginning, and that much worse is to come."

The way he ended his little speech sent most of the counsellors reeling; the idea that they were at war still had not stuck in their minds. "We break now, for you are all weary and in need of sustenance. We meet here again tomorrow at the break of dawn: there are many things still to consider and to plan for. Go now, to your well-earned repose, and have a quiet and restful night." With these words the assembly dissolved and made their way to their own private chambers or lodgings. All, that is, except Mojastic and Myra, who remained standing in the council chamber without speaking, looking inward in themselves, as it were, perhaps searching for answers.

Elderanna walked slowly back towards her cottage. Normally, she would have had a spring in her steps, but now…she just couldn't find it in her heart. The monstrous idea of war stuck in her mind and made her feel beside herself with worry. Her thoughts kept churning in her mind, helpless and bewildered, and it was not until she reached her garden where her saplings grew quietly in its deep calm surroundings, that she felt a measure of calm and reason returning. She was worried, yes, and rightly so, but she was now able to consider things from different angles and look at their options as these presented themselves to her. After taking good care of her flowers and saplings, she went into her cottage, now confident of her choices and intent on sleep: she needed it, as she seldom had before.

When General Rajan came into the open air at last, he drew it into his lungs like a man on the verge of drowning. Being cooped up inside was not for him. Sure enough, he understood the need for deliberation before action, but why did the advisors need so many words? He shook his head, smiling a little at himself. He understood them very well actually. His mind was also overwhelmed by the thought of everything that had been revealed to them this afternoon.

He walked briskly along the castle wall, coming to a barred gate. Hailing him was a young soldier by the name of Rhiann. "Hello, general. Good night, isn't it? Quiet and calm it is, like a lake in the moonlight." He smiled warmly at General Rajan and the general couldn't help but smile back.

"Yes," he said in return, "surely a blessed night." He did not, with even the slightest quirk in his voice or face, let the soldier know what went through his mind as they spoke together. Coming into his sparse quarters, however, he had a stony expression on his face. His mind was racing, counting out all that would have to be done in order to get the kingdom ready for…what? He could not even begin to fathom what they were going to be up against, the only thing he was sure of, was that they were in for a very rough time.

Going to a stool placed in front of his bed, he wrung his leather shirt off and threw it to the floor, and then he sat down and took off his boots. He stretched his long legs and sighed with content. It was always good to come back at this time of night and stretch out his limbs, relishing in the freedom of his solitude. He walked into the bathroom, and when he came back, he was as naked as the room itself, with the night air giving him little pleasant goose bumps all over his skin as he walked to the fireplace. There, right in front of the roaring flames, was the only item of luxury that he allowed himself; a huge pelt, from a gigantic bear by the look of it that covered the whole area in front of the fire, looking inviting, soft and warm. It was all that, and Rajan smiled softly to himself as he lowered his body, lean and strong, onto the pelt. Still smiling, he was asleep in only a few minutes.

With the shocked gasps of her advisors ringing in her ears, her eyes met the eyes of the soothsayer. They were wide and scared but showed no sign of the shock that were present in the eyes of everyone else around the table. Instead, they looked sad and—somehow—embittered. And knowing— terribly knowing, if anyone knew what lay in store for them, she was the one to ask. The soothsayer stood up and took the stage, ending the confused babble around the room. She looked at them gravely and slowly she began to talk. Her words sent shivers down their backs even though it was high summer, and by the time she was finished, more than one of them were openly crying while the others fought a battle with their tears…

The next morning dawned, nice and clear, without a trace of the horrors she had encountered in the night. Nevertheless, she knew that the time was here. She took a long, last look around her, taking in everything, drinking it in as if filled with an unquenchable thirst. Then, closing the view of her land and people in her heart forever, she set out on her journey—a journey from which she would never return.

Chapter 4
A Fresh Start

In the now empty council chamber Mojastic and Myra looked at each other for a long time. Then they both started speaking at once, as so often happens in such situations, they halted, made a fresh start—once again at the same time—laughed a little, and then Mojastic gestured that Myra should speak first; she was after all a lady. She smiled and bowed her head in recognition of his good manners, then opened the conversation simply by asking him, "Where am I supposed to sleep? I can feel the weight of this day lying heavy on my shoulders and I would like nothing more than a few hours of repose."

Mojastic smiled in return, "An apartment has been made ready for you," he said, "and the servants are awaiting your arrival there shortly." He then offered her his arm and together they walked slowly through the quiet and sleepy castle. They took their time, talking about this and that: the flowers and crops in the castle gardens—both looking to be splendid, the fish in the lakes and the river, the forests teeming with wildlife, and other topics of nature and life, topics that were pleasantly free of all references to sorcerers or war. The walk was therefore a pleasant one, and Mojastic found himself sorry that it had to come to an end. But as they entered the part of the castle where the apartments lay, he regretfully told Myra that this was her quarters and that he bade her a good night. For a fraction of a second, she just looked at him, then said, "Will you not join me? For I am not used to eating alone and your company is very pleasant to me."

Mojastic's heart almost leapt out of his chest at that, and he hardly found breath enough to tell her, "I most certainly will if that is what you wish!"

This is how the romance of Mojastic and Myra began—a romance that would reverberate through time and light up the gloomiest room when told. From her cabin on the outskirts of the wood, Elderanna could see the brightly lit windows of the apartment where she knew Myra had been installed. She could also see the dark windows where Mojastic had his abode, and she knew that he was not in his rooms, hence the lack of light. Smiling to herself, she followed the proceedings from her own window while knitting socks for youngsters in the village—there were always children who needed socks. When at last the lights were extinguished in Myra's apartment, and no presence or light had been detected in Mojastic's chambers, she sighed in relief and put down her needles. Smiling secretively to herself, she went about making herself a little late snack and then headed for bed, satisfied that some things were right at least, and the line of kings would be continued.

The next morning dawned bright and clear—as clear as one could possibly wish for—and without even a hint of things being amiss. But amiss they were, nonetheless, and Elderanna knew this perhaps better than anyone else in Arboria. She had been watching nature around her for a long time, studying it closely, and she had seen the signs: dying plant life, faltering animal life, corroding stones and rocks, moss growing slimier and stickier, grass being coarser and less nutritious than before and so on and on. In sum, she was witnessing—in infinitesimal steps at a time—the decline of nature all around her. But it was not just the elements in her surroundings, it was also the core of the people's soul that was being corroded: their lifeforce so to speak. People's faces were looking haggard and drawn—not so much that you would notice it from day to day, but when you met someone whom you had not seen for a while, then it hit you. People looked as if they were not sleeping and eating well; they were getting thinner and they seemed like shadows of themselves. She puffed and sighed to herself as she was brewing a cup of tea—apples and cinnamon, her very favourite, and from a good yard and year too. Lifting her face to the sun and sniffing the air, for a moment she felt like a lass of sixteen again, then she smiled a little at the thought; sixteen was long gone, if she had ever been there…and went inside to get her breakfast—a small slice of bread roasted over the fire and topped with fresh, green herbs from her garden. It was not too long before the trumpets sounded the beginning of a new day from the castle walls and shortly after the bell sounded for the council to meet again.

The council members, as they entered the council chamber, had a somewhat haggard look, but this was rectified by the excellent breakfast that was provided. Even Elderanna was tempted and ended up eating a second breakfast consisting of fruits and delicious white bread that had been baked that same morning. Then they set to work again, and this time they were all focused on the tasks immediately ahead of them: sending envoys to the surrounding kingdoms, gathering intelligence from both official and other sources, and starting to weave a web of protection around the people and land of Arboria. As they had established that there was a malign will behind the occurrences which they all had experienced, it was now time to come up with some countermeasures. This last task was by far the most complicated or complex, not to mention the most dangerous. The members of the council involved in this venture, were all of them versed in the arts of enchantment and casting of spells—some of them more than others—but it still provided them with many challenges and obstacles along the way. Elderanna was part of this group, as well as Myra and two of the councilmen who were advisors, but also solid spell casters. To her surprise, Myra found that Mojastic joined the group as well. Looking enquiringly at Elderanna, she made a little nod towards Mojastic. Elderanna looked at him thoughtfully for a second, then addressed him, "Sir, will you be joining us? I didn't know you had an interest in magic?"

Mojastic looked at her with a distinct twinkle in his eye, "Well, I would say that there might be a thing or two about me that has escaped your roving and searching eye over the years!" Then he became serious, "I have always been interested in magic, or spellcasting anyways, but there has never been any occasion for me to try it and not be detected, so to speak. Now, however, we have got to use spells, and I will do what I can to help." With that, he sat down in the circle that had been formed by the spell casters. Myra was looking intently at him and he turned his head to her, "With your permission, of course," he said, and the tone of his voice was so new to everyone there that they all turned to look at him.

The truth of what was happening then hit them all, more or less at the same time, and the room lit up as they smiled knowingly to themselves and each other. But it only lasted for a brief moment before the seriousness of the situation sobered them up.

When the clock struck noon and the bell tolled again, the council recessed for an hour to get some rest and refreshments. Myra and Mojastic left together with their heads bowed close in earnest conversation. They seemed to have many things weighing on their minds at present and not all of them unpleasant. Elderanna took a shortcut across the courtyard and into the kitchens. There were three kitchens in the castle: one bakery, one for the main courses and one for desserts, cakes and sweets. It was to the bakery that she made her way, weaving back and forth to avoid getting trampled on or getting in the way of the cooks that were present at this time of the day. The bakers started earliest of them all, she knew, for they were responsible for the loads of bread and rolls required to keep the inhabitants of the castle marching, or at least working. At this hour, a good few of them were in bed, getting some sleep, but fresh manpower had been awakened and was going at their job with full vigour, due to special orders issued by the king. Now they were baking pastries, dinner rolls and pies for the evening meal. When Elderanna poked into the kitchen they all smiled and winked at her.

In the big main course kitchen, everybody was working, in fact it would be safe to say that all hands were on deck and working flat out! It reminded her of a beehive: just as jostling, busy and hurried, but—like the beehive—in an organised way. They were frantic to get all the different dishes ready, for the king had announced that a very special occasion was forthcoming and all the courtiers, ladies, farmers, and craftsmen in town as well as the villages, were invited to be there and partake in their festivities.

Finally, she checked in on the dessert kitchen, and if the other two kitchens had been busy, she could not rightly say what this kitchen was. It was a wonder that the head chef's head did not explode in the cacophony. It was total mayhem, or at least it seemed that way, but after some time it emerged as slightly more organised chaos! Shaking her head, she re-emerged on the courtyard and set her course for the cool shadows of the library were Ingan and Tarlief—the two advisors in the spellcasting group—were waiting. They had some serious studying to do before the afternoon session!

"Although the magic that these folks had was crude, it was efficient and strong, and she felt relieved at the thought that they would help in the struggle to come. If only there had been more of them! But she saw now that they were determined to do their part, and if her powers of judging character had not failed her, then she also knew that these people would not flinch back nor stand down in battle! Her task felt less like a sacrifice now, and more like an adventure. One without hope of return, but an adventure just the same!"

Chapter 5
The Spells Are Cast,
the Dice Are Rolled

As the council recommenced after their break, their proceedings took on an even more serious note. It was time for strategies to be forged and measures to be taken. The whole day had been used for preparations and now it was time for the spell casting to begin, for the malign force to be turned, beaten or at least held in check with what magic they possessed. The rest of the council stepped aside as a small group of five people with Mojastic in the lead walked solemnly up the stairs to the high turret of the castle. The platform on top was a sizeable one, going the whole way around the tower and offering room enough for the entire party with plenty to spare. From there they could see for miles in every direction—a truly magnificent view of the surrounding countryside.

Myra was the first to throw her spells into the air. Lifting her hands above her head and throwing her face up to the light of the sun, she looked like an ancient sun-goddess basking in the rays. Her hands seemed to weave thin threads from the sun's rays, knitting them together in a fine spider web that shone like bands of exquisite silk, fluttering and swaying on the light breeze. As she worked, this web stretched out over the kingdom, filling the air over their heads, extending further and further, until it reached the very borders of Arboria. There it lightly touched down and fused with the ground and became a glittering dome, one which malign entities and persons could not enter, but which let through everything and everyone else. In fact, they did not even notice the dome, for once it had been put into place it faded away and became invisible.

Ingan, one of the advisors who were also a spellcaster, was next, and he looked as if he had had second thoughts, but as bailing out was not an option, he had decided to stand his ground. His voice, a clear tenor, was raised suddenly up to the clouds in the high skies with a spell to bring confusion and disorientation on those who tried to enter the kingdom with ill intent. It took a while to complete, and when he was finished, he almost collapsed. He was followed by Tarlief, yet another of the advisors and spellcaster, who dealt with the forces in the ground: the rocks and stones and turf and bones of the earth. It too took quite a while, and now the light in the sky was becoming golden in hue.

For a moment, the world held its breath, and then another stepped forward to do his part. Mojastic lifted his hands as if he beckoned the whole world to listen, and then he began to chant. With a deep, melodious voice, he held them all enthralled while he laid an enchantment on the land, one that would hold the malice away from their doorstep, one that would ensure that no ill will or thought could enter their dreams and poison their hearts. While it lasted, he also held everyone in a spell so strong that some of them forgot to breathe, amongst them Myra. Already deeply intertwined with him and his fate, she was still shocked to find that he had such power and had never used it before. The moment seemed to hang forever in the air, but it ended eventually, and while they all resumed their normal breathing Elderanna stepped forward as the last of the group. The stars were out by now, faintly blinking in the clear unstained sky, and the sun was sinking slowly through an ocean of green trees.

Although being the smallest in the group, she was far from the frailest. She stood in the middle of the open space, quite still, as if she was listening to something that the others could not hear. Then she began, "Winds of the world; grant us smooth days and quiet nights. Water of the air; give us moist earth and good yield. Earth that provides; bring us the sustenance which we need. Fire in the heart; grant us the courage to battle that which lies ahead. For the world is changing and the wheel is turning, and the lives we have been leading are past." Then she straightened her back and appeared almost to grow before their eyes. Tall and imposing she looked, like a queen, but one from the elder days, when the world was young. And her voice lifted above the world, surpassing the boundaries of a human voice, encompassing all that lived and breathed under the sky, gathering everything into one huge cry, "Rhanddemarr, I say unto you, 'Begone from this world, begone. For I condemn you to the eternal darkness if you do not forego this venture!'"

Nature fell silent, eerily silent, and even the stars seemed to stand still. The world held its breath and for a minute. Myra thought she was going to faint, but then...the answer came, and a voice never heard before rang out. Cold it was, colder than the eternal frost in the tundra, colder than the glaciers of

Mount Dorth, colder even than the universe at its coldest. And it was soft as down, but steely as a sword, and with jagged edges like shards of broken glass. It terrified them all and turned even the strongest and bravest into weak-kneed saplings. "I hear you, withered hag from the river fields, and I resent your command. This time it is you who will be gone from this world, you and all that rubble you have trailing after you. You will all be cast from this world, but I will not disclose your destination! For I am Rhanddemarr and I will not stand for the kind of insolence you are displaying!" With that, there came a bolt of lightning that seemed to cleave the sky in two, but by good chance it did not strike the castle of Arboria or even the land surrounding it; perhaps it was their enchantments and magic that turned it away. But there was, however, a casualty—or so it seemed. When their eyesight was restored, they saw Elderanna lying on the deck, motionless and still. They rushed to her aid and tried to comfort her as best they could, but it felt like an age went by before she stirred and opened her eyes. Mojastic stared into those eyes, long and hard, to look for any and all evidence of a foreign will, but in the end he relaxed. She smiled apologetically to them and said, "That was a blast that I did not expect. Next time around, he will not find me so easy to throw down!" With that she clambered to her feet, and amid much cheering and clamouring, she and the others went down again from the tower and entered the courtyard.

When they came down, they found the people in an uproar: everyone was scared and upset and the air was buzzing with questions about what had happened, but they quickly settled down when Mojastic stood up and told them that, although they had gotten an unpleasant surprise up on the roof, everything was now okay. He then issued an invitation to the whole town and all the surrounding villages to join them for an announcement and evening of festivities, before dissembling the council for the moment. Each of the council members went to their own quarters and rested and prepared themselves for the evening and the meal they were about to partake in.

Elderanna went to her cabin, slowly and somewhat laboriously. She was aching all over from the bolt of lightning. True, it had not struck her, and yet she felt as if it had. Her body was weak and shaking, her mind was tired and confused, and her spirit was wavering under the weight of this new knowledge. She was his adversary and always had been, but how could this be? How could he know her? What history did they have that had earned his scorn and hatred? She was damned if she knew, but these questions would have to be answered, and fast. If not, she would be at a serious disadvantage at their next meeting.

"We were so easily beaten!" The thought had taken hold in her mind and was hammering in her skull like a thousand blacksmiths, all pounding away. She could not fathom what went down on the tower, nor did she understand where this animosity did come from? And why did this wizard show such strong feeling of resentment towards Elderanna? The questions were swirling around her till she felt dizzy and nauseous. When she added to this all the drain, she had been subject to in her own ordeal with the malign will, not to mention the unexpected pang of worry for Mojastic when he stood there, tall and brave in the face of terror, it was no

wonder she was tired and confused. But her mind kept returning to the first thought, "We were so easily beaten!"

On the heels of that thought, however, came another, related but entirely different one, "How incredibly brave, courageous, strong and yet soft and gentle he was!" Standing there, erect in the middle of what seemed like a million hailstorms he was the picture of calm and authority. And he was attractive to her—there was no way of fooling herself— she was infatuated with him. Although her plan had been to join with the leader of Arboria to make a union with them, she had not expected this. It made the prophecy harder to bear and at the same time less unbearable…

Rhanddemarr's thoughts were fuming. The cold hatred he felt for Elderanna, as she called herself, was almost choking him, and the words with which he wanted to condemn her clogged in his throat until he could not draw breath. She, the wretched witch, the abominable woman that had scorned him! And now she was there yet again, thwarting his plans and destroying his opening game! He would deal with her, yes, and sooner rather than later, for he felt that she might be a danger to his plans and tactics…

And he had failed to kill this Myra—the little elf-thing— that irked him. But he would get her, soon enough, and hopefully that would put an end to the unification project they had going, she and that Mojastic fellow. And what was he about? Some upstart from the woodland realm, probably half ape. He snickered, it sounded ominous in the great hall where he was. And then there were Ordovan, Trecon, and Rajan; three more of these idiots that only went to serve as fodder for his creatures. But his thoughts returned to Elderanna; how could she be got rid of, and how had she survived in the first place?

Chapter 6
The Revelation
and a Promise

Although they had been subjected to a terrifying spectacle that afternoon, the people of Arboria still turned up in the evening. All of them were dressed in their very best, and they were equally curious and nervous, but they came, nevertheless. Somewhat subdued they entered the Great Hall where they stopped, gaping in astonishment. The hall had been decorated as it had never been before, with a wide array of various plants, flowers and birds, all of them arranged in such a way as to give the impression of being in a forest. But no one could remember ever seeing a forest quite like this one. It had trees that bore blue flowers and red moss with small yellow saplings. There were different hues of grass, from green and yellow to brown and red, and even purple! And the birds! They were flying freely around the room, and the windows were open so they could leave whenever they felt inclined to do so, but those that did take a trip outside, quickly returned to sing in the trees and entertain and awe the guests. Their feathers shone in every conceivable colour, and when they lifted their wings, they sent rainbows quivering through the air. It was truly magnificent, and something never seen before in Arboria, or anywhere else for that matter!

And the music! Soft, intricate tones blending together played on outlandish instruments mixed and interspersed with folk instruments from Arboria. It made a music that sounded as if it was coming from the outer spheres, while at the same time belonging by the fireside in a small woodland cottage—both homely and at the same time adventurous. It was a magnificent spectacle, and it left the guests stunned and awed for a long time. But eventually, of course, the spell loosened its grip, and they found their feet (and tongues) again, and the chatter that broke out was like being in the world's largest henhouse—where to top it off, the fox has just been and done the can-can! In this mayhem, Elderanna walked slowly into the hall and stood gazing at the revelries. She was smiling a little to herself, as if she had a secret, and was merely taking in the sights and sounds of the crowd of people, now waiting eagerly for the evening's main event—the one they had all come here for: Mojastic's reason or reasons for this feast. They were expecting a proclamation—or perhaps a revelation—of sorts, but what about? Everyone was curious about what he would have to say, and they all waited anxiously for his arrival.

While she stood there waiting, Elderanna wondered about the decorations and entertainment. If it had been ordered a month before, she did not think it would have been practically possible, and this was decided the same morning??? The only explanation she had, was that it was the work of an extremely powerful spell, but who…? The revelation dawned on her as Mojastic appeared at last.

When Mojastic finally arrived, with Myra by his side, he was accompanied by trumpets and calls of 'Hurray!' He stepped into the hall and everything went quiet, even the incessant twittering of the birds. Only the fountains that were hidden in the thickets went on playing their sweet music. He stepped up to the throne upon a dais at the end of the hall. Beside his throne was another, slightly more delicate, and it was to this that he led Myra. Reaching the dais, they turned and bowed to their audience, which led to a round of applause from the gathering. Their smiles beaming at the people, they sat down and accepted the thunderous applause that washed over them. When the applause started to lose its intensity, Mojastic stood up and raised his arm, "Thank you all for this welcome. It is most heartening to see your faces and hear your appraisal! Now, I want to give you some news, and I will start with a proclamation I never imagined I would have to make… For many years, we have been in a state of war with our neighbour in the north—Rhanddemarr the Sage—although it has never been spoken of, or even been present in most people's consciousness. This war has so far been one of minds, with the battles consisting of sneaking into people's dreams and entering their thoughts on a subconscious level. You have not been aware of it, only felt its effect as a cold shiver or a chill to the marrow. In short, it has been a sneaky campaign from our adversary to demoralise and dishearten us." At this, the people stared at him, first in disbelief, and then in stunned recognition, as if something crucial had just been revealed to them. After just a moment, he went on, "Today that changed. Everything changed, and our futures have been bound to a past we cannot remember, or even access. Our mortal foe, for he is nothing less, holds a grudge against this world, for reasons we still are trying to fathom, and he wants to rule everything according to his own plans and wishes. We have learned that this is not a grudge that he holds to our people alone, or even specifically, he holds a grudge against all the world's peoples and his war has been waged against every single one of them. This afternoon we went up to the platform of the highest tower in the palace, to see if we could somehow feel the extent of the power that we suspected was behind this. We got more than we bargained for, with the lightning stroke that seemed to cover our country in his wrath. Elderanna bore the brunt of his anger, and I am very pleased to see that she has been given no lasting harm." At this, another round of applause broke out.

Eventually, this also died down, and Mojastic continued, "At last, we have heard the voice of Rhanddemarr, and his words—though chilling—were nevertheless almost a relief to hear, for now we know whereas before we guessed. From his words it became clear what he wants from us. He demands that we all yield and accept him as our overlord and supreme ruler, or we will end in misery and despair worse even than our worst and darkest dreams and nightmares can possibly show us! Needless to say, we rejected his bidding and will continue to do so, even were we alone. But we do not stand alone! By my side stand Myra Horathion from the land of Afamia. They have long endured the malicious advances of said sorcerer, but now they have come to a point when they can no longer stand alone. Our experiment today showed us beyond doubt that this is the case for more than Afamia; it concerns all the lands in our region—at least. Perhaps it is even more widespread, but as I speak, envoys have been dispatched to our immediate neighbours. They are to present the threat and call for a council of kings and queens, and to ask for a swift reply." At this, the stunned faces in the crowd became animated again, and many started cheering and clapping their hands over their heads. Mojastic lifted his right hand and they fell quiet once again, "I know this is grim news to you, and for most of us—who have never known war—it is the beginning of times of uncertainty and worry. But in the middle of these troubling thoughts I have also one piece of news that I hope will make your hearts soar the way it has made mine: Myra Horathion has conceded to be my wife!" As soon as had he spoken these words, the congregation gathered there broke out in calls, singing, shouting and thunderous applause once again. It was regular mayhem, and no one could make them quiet down. The tsunami of revelries went on and on, as if it never would stop, and seemed to intensify rather than die out. But, eventually, it did, or at least became less intense. Mojastic, smiling down from the dais with Myra by his side, seemed genuinely happy and very much in love. "This union," he said, "will not only strengthen our defences, Myra being an accomplished enchantress, but it will in fact unite our two kingdoms, with her also being the queen of Afamia!" This time a bystander would have thought that the roof was caving in with the noise, applause, stomping, and hollering! Cries of "Yes!" and "Long live the king and queen!" echoed throughout the hall.

Elderanna, who had been watching the proceedings from the back of the hall, now made her way to the front of the throng, beaming broadly to the couple on the dais. "Well, well," she said, shaking her head. "This was an eye-opener! Not the news about your marriage, of course, that has been in the making since the moment you two met. But you," she said, turning to Myra, "You kept your true standing well-hidden from all, including me, and I am not easily duped! It was clear to me that you were royalty, but the queen!" She appeared to be strict, but there was a twinkle in her eyes that belied this, and when she could not hold her chuckles in anymore, her laughter rang strong and free through the palace. Elderanna was clearly not displeased with being played in this matter, and the people laughed with her. On this note the festivities of the evening were commenced and lasted until well after the sun rose the following morning.

When the sun broke over the mountaintops, it found them all gathered in the courtyard, looking up towards the pinnacle of the tower where two figures stood, holding hands. As the sun rose in the sky, slowly and majestically, it gilded them until they looked completely shining and alien, just floating in a golden mist. Then they raised their hands and intertwined their fingers—seemingly inside the sun—and, when the crowd cheered, they were engulfed in the sun's rays. Blinking their eyes against the strong sunlight, the crowd at first thought they had disappeared, but then they came into the field of vision once more, now clad all in white and gold, and with belts of spun gold around their waists. *Finally,* Elderanna thought, *finally he is home!*

That afternoon the council met again, still dazed and happy on account of the events that had taken place, and none were smiling more than the main attractions: Mojastic and Myra. Nevertheless, they still had some decisions to make before they could begin to take action or make decisive plans for how they should proceed. Their first priority, warning their neighbours, had already been seen to and the envoys were on their way. The second, forging an alliance to battle their enemy, was begun, but just barely, and it would take some time before they were ready with this. The third priority, ordering things at home to be ready for more direct attacks, was on the agenda for the day, and this task had many burning questions inside it. They were the bulwark against the sorcerer, not by choice, but by sheer bad luck it seemed. How were they going to use this to their advantage? How could they organise a defence against an enemy when they knew next to nothing about him? What measures could be taken to ensure the safety of the villagers that lived outside the city walls? Could these people be protected at all, or would they have to be moved inside? Was the military force they had, strong enough to fight the enemy, or would it have to be reinforced? And to this last question, what could they be reinforced with that could be at help to them in their struggles?

The questions were many and so far, they did not have a single answer. Mojastic, however, was determined that this situation was going to change—one way or the other he was going to find some answers to build his plans on! His first action was to order books from the library. But none of his advisors, generals or even Elderanna had even heard of the volumes that he requested, 'Silent Warcraft', 'Haunted Swords,' 'The art of the magi' and 'Hexing Stones' were among the titles that were called for. "I do not recall seeing any of these volumes in the library," muttered one of the advisors, a strong, but grumpy or sour-looking man of about fifty years. This was Arcull, and he had only recently been named advisor.

"That," said Mojastic, "would be because these books are not in the library per se. They are locked up in a chamber below the castle and kept under guard there, not be seen by unwary or spying eyes." He continued, "I myself have not looked at them before, but I know some of what is supposed to be in them and suspect we can find some things of use to us in our present predicament." Then he divided the assembly into four groups and gave them all the same assignment: To read through the book or books that were put before them, then decide whether it contained something useful to them and make notes for later discussions. When this was settled, they all went to work.

Hours went by as they struggled with unfamiliar wording and strange script, but nightfall came and still they kept at it, turning the pages as they went along. The task was made even more difficult by the fact that many of the books did not contain a register or table of contents. Still they kept a steady pace, and when Mojastic called for a break, they were well past midnight and into the small hours of the night. Mojastic told them to get some rest and return to work after breakfast. It would not be a long rest—breakfast was only five hours away—but one sorely needed. Still, the gravity of the situation and the lingering feeling of panic that had been instilled in them by their excursion and experiences on the roof, now fresh in their brains once more, made them want to ignore him and plod on. It was only when Elderanna spoke up and told them that they would be able to speed up their work and make it more efficient with a little rest that they conceded and went to their quarters.

Rajan and Elderanna walked through the door together when she thought she noticed something odd in the general's demeanour. Looking intently at him she asked him what was afoot and the answer she got betrayed the fact that he was struggling to make sense of the events. He said, "I do not like to sound impatient or eager for war—heavens know, I know what war is! But this war is bewildering and frustrating for someone like me: A foe I cannot see and battles I cannot win!"

Chuckling softly and somewhat bitterly she touched his arm, "I know exactly how you feel, and believe me, this is very frustrating for us all. But you needn't worry, before long I predict that there will be solid foes to meet and fights and battles that must be won—more than even a veteran like yourself can stomach!" Startled, he looked at her confused for a second, then his face cleared and smiling a little, they parted and went each to their own quarters.

After a short and somewhat broken period of sleep they were at it again: reading, evaluating, discussing and sometimes trying out different spells and incantations. Some proved to be hopeful, some showed instant promise and most, sadly, did not.

After one of those unsuccessful ventures, which ended up with quite a few headaches and bruises on the people involved, they took a brief break from the library and got some fresh air. Myra was one of those nursing a sore head, and she breathed deeply the sweet scent of woodlands and flowers after the hours spent in the company of old, dusty and mouldy books. Elderanna kept her company as they strolled around a secluded garden nearly hidden behind the castle. They spoke in gentle voices about the beauty of the scenery and kept well away from the topic that had so clouded their minds during the last days. Birds were singing while a squirrel was busy clearing out the nest and preparing for the imminent arrival of new younglings. A brook was babbling happily among the trees, chuckling lively to itself as it rushed towards the river in the bottom of the valley. That river would become a flood before it reached the ocean—leagues upon leagues away. The birds and insects did not appear to have a care in the world, and it was tempting to let go and be just as free and relaxed—to just not think and to pretend that their worries were figments of their imaginations. But there was a question that was gnawing Elderanna's mind—had been for the last days anyway: What was there behind Myra's words about Mojastic in the war chamber? Finally, Elderanna found the opening she was looking for, and taking a deep breath, she dared to ask Myra directly, "If I'm not too forward, I would like to ask you a question that has been gnawing at me for the last days—it won't let me rest properly and is always at the back of my mind."

Myra looked at her questioningly. "If there is anything, I can do to alleviate your burden, don't hesitate to ask," she said.

"I will answer as best I can."

"Well," said Elderanna, "it is personal, so I can understand if you do not want to answer, but I have a feeling it is going to be important for the unfolding of events as we go along." By now, Myra was curious and so she urged her on.

"When we first spoke, you indicated that you had a task ahead of you that the king—now your husband—was going to make both easier and harder for you. What exactly did you refer to?" Elderanna looked into her eyes and held them, waiting for the answer. It was slow in coming, and Elderanna was almost holding her breath, lest she startle Myra in her thoughtfulness.

At last, she took a breath and said, "I haven't told you everything about the background for why I came. I could have sent an envoy, except... I couldn't." She looked directly at Elderanna with tears sparkling in her eyes. "There is a prophecy involved, a prophecy both grim and hopeful at the same time. It stated that, 'a queen from the land of the winged shall carry the child of a king from the woods.'" She paused, then continued, "After the child is born, the winged one shall fade away, carried on a flood of tears, while the light of the world shall grow from her ashes." She turned her face quickly away from Elderanna's shocked countenance.

Slowly Elderanna reached out and touched Myra on the shoulder, "No," she whispered, "no, it cannot be! Why would you find love like this only to sacrifice yourself on the altar of destiny? How can the gods of fate ask you to do such a thing? How???"

"It is fate," Myra answered in a strange, choked voice, "and I have to play my part. The only thing I had not reckoned with, was me getting feelings for this woodland king. He is kind and caring, and at the same time he can be stern and proud, and he has talents that go way on the outside of anything I ever expected in a king. The smile on his face and the laughter in his eyes, masks unfathomable depths in his mind, depths where he stores all his experiences, all his learning and everything he observes, to ponder on it and devise his philosophy from it. He is a little boy, a young man, a wise sage, and an ancient philosopher—all in one."

"And he's yours—body and soul—for eternity," Elderanna whispered. "I have never seen him so immersed in anyone or anything before, he's like a child reborn!"

Myra turned and smiled at her, and although her tears were falling, she still managed to look happy. "I know," she said simply. Silence fell between them, a silence full of words that would not allow themselves to be uttered, words of care, sorrow and joy that were nevertheless spoken in their minds.

Together they stood there in silence, while the world revolved around them—happy, noisy and as jubilant as ever.

Where had all these emotions been hiding??? Mojastic was overwhelmed by the sheer strength of the love he felt. It was as if he had come to life seconds ago, and all his life before this moment, he had been dreaming. Myra was...she was extraordinary in every way: beautiful, intelligent, cool-headed, smart, strong, and caring. And probably more characteristics, too, he thought to himself. He was feeling stunned, overjoyed, gentlemanly, soft, tongue-tied and honey-tongued at the same time... But amidst the confusion these emotional tides brought with them, he also felt calm: a serenity beyond anything he had ever felt before, and he knew: she was his soul mate, his forever love. Without her presence this world meant nothing, he would be dead inside if he had to face the world alone after meeting her, knowing her—dead!

Chapter 7
Nightfall

Upon returning to the council chamber, they found the council members present, in an agitated state. In the middle of the room—seated on one of the chairs—was a messenger from the queen of Terafuma, Sashe. He had apparently just arrived and was breathing laboriously in ragged gasps. Myra looked at him, silently wondering what could have made him so out of breath or rushed him so badly that his capacity was quite spent. Sensing that someone looked at her, she turned and saw Mojastic's eyes—grave and weary—looking back. As servants came bustling in with food, wine and medication for the man, Mojastic turned his attention to the council again.

"As you can see, the first of our envoys have already been answered," said he, "or rather they crossed each other's paths as our envoy had not yet arrived when this messenger set out on his journey. But that is not relevant. What is of concern is that Terafuma has experienced many of the same occurrences as we have, and they have sent out envoys to their neighbours just as we have done. The only strategy, they have not employed yet, is trying out the enemy's strength and protect the people from his power. This has proved disastrous for them: three out of every ten people—all army—have fallen under the 'screaming sickness': whenever they fall asleep, the dreams they encounter make them scream fit to raise the dead and—of course—rob everyone in their proximity of their sleep in turn. This happened before our attempt at weaving a protective web over Arboria, so there is no connection between the events as such. Nevertheless, we have had a narrow escape!"

Amid the gasps and mutterings around the room, a voice was raised, "What are we going to do?" It was General Rajan, now accompanied by his fellow generals; Ordovan and Trecon—of the engineer's corps and the river corps, respectively. They looked at Mojastic with identical looks of determination and eagerness on their faces—eagerness to see action and determination to win, both of which were good traits in a general.

Mojastic acknowledged them with a nod before replying, "We are going to send help in the form of spell casters—I am sending Ingan and Tarlief—to help remedy the situation. In addition, we are going to deploy a force to help with border patrol until the soldiers in their army are back on their feet again."

The generals nodded in unison and asked to be released so they could sit down and plan for the taskforce that would be sent off. Time was of importance—it was necessary to get going as quick as possible, given the fact that the borders of Terafuma were sadly understaffed at present. General Rajan was to go with the force and order things to the best for everyone, in cooperation with his Terafumian counterpart, General Amlon.

Then Mojastic turned to matters relating to Arboria, "We have tried out several angles and spells in our attempts to find something of use to us. We have found a few good ones—as well as a massive number of spells with little or no effect—and the good ones we will now put into motion. This will be done to strengthen our defences, heighten our alarm system, and prepare our counterattack measures. I—for one—sincerely hope that we will never have to go to the length of attacking our opponent, but sometimes attack is the best defence, and so we must be prepared to strike first—if necessary." He looked sternly at each and everyone in the room, looking them straight in the eyes and holding their gaze until he got the answer he was looking for. Not all of them were ready at once; some needed a moment to weigh the pros and cons in their mind before their resolve solidified. *You have to bear in mind that the situation is totally new and frightening to all of them,* Mojastic thought. And there were some that faltered. Grimor and Arcull were not ready to give Mojastic the support he was looking for, but for entirely different reasons. Their reasons were veiled in their minds, behind the walls of their countenances, and were not revealed in their voices when at last they signalled their consent.

When Mojastic spoke again, he did so to dole out the tasks at hand for everyone, "Myra, Elderanna, and Ingan and Tarlief upon their return, will join me in the council for magical measures. Our job will be to have a constant vigilance and presence on the borders of Arboria and the surrounding lands—an early warning system if you will. Also, we will participate in all skirmishes and acts of war, providing such protection as can be given to our troops. We will work closely together with my three generals—Rajan, Ordovan and Trecon—to ensure that our protection measures will be as full and effective as we can make them. Methena, Joghartha and

Porlene will, together with Grimor as the eldest, take care of the business of daily life—provisions, farming needs, schools, housing and clothing—ordering and looking after all the little things that are so essential for a good life despite the situation. Arcull will run the administration of the castle. Has everyone understood what their role is going to be?" People nodded affirmatively, and subsequently went to their jobs with a look of grim determination and resolve on their faces.

Turning to the little council that was left, Mojastic said, smiling sardonically, "Well, ladies, who would like another trip up to the tower with me?"

Looking grave, but with a smile in her eyes, Myra replied, "I'd go anywhere with you, my lord." But they both knew it would be somewhat less than enjoyable…

As the day was nearing nightfall, they found themselves on the platform again, gathering their wits about them and calling on the spirits and forces of nature as they went about strengthening the defences and setting up a form of early warning system that would alert them to any untoward movements or alien forces in the proximity of their borders. When their job was finally done, nightfall had come in earnest and darkness was descending over the castle, sending its fingers creeping up the walls. Exhausted they stumbled down the stairs and slumped into chairs in the private hall of the king. As they sat there in silence, looking at each other, Mojastic noticed that Elderanna was looking sad and serious while resting her eyes somewhere in the distance. Upon his asking how she felt, however, she did not say anything untoward or reveal anything that might be the source of her uneasiness, and so he let the matter rest, for now at least. At last, they stood up, and bidding each other a good night and wishing each other a quiet rest, Mojastic and Myra went to their chamber while Elderanna walked to her hut, relishing the quiet and warm night that crept about her like a soft blanket. She was weary, yes, and shocked by what she had been told this afternoon, but at the same time a new resolve had awakened in her, and she was now determined to see this through, no matter what.

Oh, she thought, *it is a good thing people do not know what lies in store in the future.* By this time she had reached her hut, and once she was in the seclusion of her own home, she let down her guard and let her tears flow freely, "But I know…" Thinking this and still crying, she fell asleep, with her tears wetting her pillow, and darkness descended.

In her dream, she was once again floating in the air above Mount Dorth, but this time—as she listened—she could hear more of what the voice was chanting, "In the depths, in the abyss, in the darkness of oblivion you were cast before the day began. Now I call you to emerge as the daylight wanes: From the depths, from the abyss, from the darkness of oblivion you shall rise like the phoenix! Rise in fury, rise in glory, rise into a blood-red sunset!"

Chapter 8
Storm Is Coming

The inhabitants of Arboria felt a bit shellshocked but being a sturdy people, they quickly regained their wits. They soon fell back to their daily routines, comings and goings, and trade and travelling inside the borders were also picking up again. As the weeks became months, and as spring unfolded around them, the days crept slowly forwards in much the same manner as always. If there were portents or omens in the air these were not detectable to the people scurrying about their daily business. Mojastic had gotten replies to all his envoys, and although they mostly were negative as to a council meeting, the council of kings and queens proved to be an impossible task to manage, they were most informative when it came to what incidents had been experienced in the different regions. The nearby countries were in varying states of turmoil and the regents had more than enough to do to manage their affairs. Also, there did not appear any solutions to their problem, but counsels were given, and advice taken, and there was great exchange of magical ideas and remedies. Although the countermeasures applied in the other countries were much the same as in Arboria, he noticed that their spell casters were not as proficient as his, or perhaps he had been a little quicker in the uptake and so prevented one or two of the attacks.

As he got a clearer picture of the development in each of the countries around him, he could make out the reach and direction of the power at play, and some of the aspects of this worried him. So much in fact, that he called for his advisors to come to the castle for a discussion. However, he had not yet disclosed anything from these meetings which had taken place with just him and one advisor at a time.

Gradually growing warmer and longer, each day seemed to contain everything imaginable for your pleasure: the sights and smells of flowers budding, corn and vegetables sown and growing, and not to forget the sounds of lambs bleating over the noise of the rivers and waterfalls, and people singing as they worked in the fields or other chores around the farms.

The sounds of joy mingled together in a symphony with never-ending cascades or waves of tones, but they were also joined by something new: a sound not heard before, or at least not very often. From every glen and open field there came the sound of arrows whistling through the air and the dull thump of them striking their targets. In addition, there was the sound of combat practise: shields clashing with swords and lances, soldiers practising one-to-one combat with knives and ropes, bola-throwing and wind-racer practice. A wind-racer worked like a boomerang, but depending on how you threw it, it could curve, fly straight or wobble, making a seesaw pattern in the air.

Another weapon was something called a 'lightning bolt'. It was a lance in appearance, but at the end it had a crystal instead of a spearhead. When it was thrust forward a bolt of electricity was released, striking the opponent. As any soldier who had had a meeting with a lightning bolt would tell you, it incapacitated any foe for a considerable amount of time! The lightning bolts that they had gotten now were decidedly stronger and more accurate than before, although at the same time they were also lighter and slenderer than the earlier versions. Depending on how much power the soldier wielded it with, it could mean anything from mild discomfort to death for the person on the receiving end, so the soldiers were told to wield them with utmost caution. In the practise fields where they tried out these weapons, the air was ripe with a smell of burnt metal, or rather a smell of electricity.

Such gatherings of the army, or at least parts of it, were not unheard of—the different details needed practise and repetition from time to time. But this was different; this time they were preparing for war in earnest and many of the soldiers wore a puzzled or dazed look on their face, as if they were dreaming and had a hard time snapping out of it.

The good news, or a part of it anyway, was that the dreams had stopped and the unrest that people had been feeling was a thing of the past. That didn't mean that it couldn't return, but at least for the moment the nights were blissfully quiet. One of the people who were relishing this respite, was Elderanna. With everything that had been happening lately, she for one needed to 'root' herself—to put her feet firmly onto—or into—the ground and bask in the feeling of being one with the great mother, as she called nature. She was doing just this when a soft knock on the doorframe of her cabin woke her up from her contemplation of a flower behind her abode. As she turned the corner to the front of the cabin, she found Myra standing there, and she was dissolved in tears.

Surprised and concerned, Elderanna quickly invited her in and ushered her through the door. Guiding Myra to a comfortable chair, she found a handkerchief which she handed to her. Myra took it with a muffled, "Thank you," and used it to wipe her eyes and face before taking the cup that Elderanna held in front of her. Taking a deep sip from it, she seemed to regain some of her usual calmness, and was at last ready to answer the questions she saw dancing in the other woman's eyes. "I…" she began, but then she faltered. A myriad of different ways to start her explanation crowded in her head, but somehow, "I'm sorry for disturbing you," seemed wrong, and, "I apologise for the hour…" seemed equally lame. In the end, she said simply, "I need your advice, sister," at which Elderanna smiled warmly.

"Of course," she said, "Tell me what it is that is clouding your otherwise bright countenance."

Smiling a little at that, Myra sipped her tea again, and then went on to explain, "I've had ill news from home: Dragon-like creatures have attacked the town and surrounding hamlets, leaving the crops burning and wasted and many dead in their wake. Also, the weather has turned completely, going from bad to worse, even killing animals with gale-force winds, pebble-sized hail and rain. They need me, more than ever, but my advisors tell me to stay put. I have a different responsibility now, and a wider goal, and I cannot let them get in the way of the greater good I am trying to achieve. But it hurts, it hurts so bad, thinking of them all in dire need and not being able to help or at least ease their plight."

Elderanna could only listen in shocked silence as Myra went on, "But the dragon attacks are not the worst. They are quickly spotted when they come swooping down and the people can defend themselves against them. But they cannot defend themselves against that which comes from the inside... Many people have died, all of them in their sleep, of a malady that they call—for lack of a better name—the 'howling demon sleep'. It seems almost like the screaming sickness which they had in Terafuma, but this is worse. People go to sleep in the evening and sleep soundly for a few hours, before suddenly sitting bolt upright while howling like a banshee. They still seem completely asleep—their eyes are closed, and they appear to be in deep slumber—but they howl like they are being tortured in the most barbaric way and their limbs contort in impossible positions until they slump down—dead. My chamber maid and close friend, Morena, was the first to die of this horrible affliction, but many have followed."

Elderanna bowed her head in sorrow and compassion. She knew all too well the feeling of being helpless in the face of death and disease: her charges did not always make it, although she was a very well accomplished healer. Still, in this situation, she had some experience. "You may not know," she said, "but this is not the first time that these maladies have been recorded. They are mentioned in one of the oldest manuscripts in Mojastic's library: Magical Ailments." Pausing, she smiled a little, then continued, "These ailments were found to have, if not a cure, then at least a remedy that would lessen the effects: the leaves of the Garusch-flower. It is rare and little known, and most people shun it because of its smell, or stink, I should say. Still, it grows in the shade of old evergreen trees and can be found flowering by the light of the moon."

Myra's eyes opened wide in surprise, "The Garusch-flower? How come I have never heard of it?"

Elderanna chuckled, "Well, there are not many who know, so it is not surprising that you have not heard of it before. Let us go into my garden and see what we may discover there. If the plant is currently in bloom, you may take some leaves and send them to your people. A small sample goes a long way, and when they know what to look for, they can find it for themselves."

The two ladies got to their feet and walked into the garden, carrying the harvesting tools with them and relishing the quiet atmosphere and calm of the flowering surroundings, making their way towards the far eastern end of it. As they walked slowly through the different patches of flowers and other plants, Myra marvelled at the abundance found in this spot. There were few places in Arboria or indeed anywhere that could compete with Elderanna's garden, in beauty, tranquillity, or usefulness. Myra looked at the myriad of colours and took in the scents of hundreds of known and unknown plants as they made their way into the shaded corner where Elderanna knew her Garusch-flowers grew. When they stood in the shade of the pine trees, Myra expected her own mood to be relaxed, but that was not the case: an almost unbelievable noxious smell, or indeed stink, overpowered her nostrils and sent her mind reeling. "Oh, my!" she said, shocked, "they really do stink!"

Elderanna laughed, "Yes, they do; potently so!"

The plant itself was considerably smaller and more anonymous than the smell of it. Tiny little blue stars in the moss, easily missed if you did not know what to look for. As they were cutting the leaves gently from the flower stems,

Myra asked Elderanna what she thought the future would be like if they did not have this foe to reckon with. Elderanna was thoughtful for a minute, and then answered, "I honestly hadn't given it much consideration. The future has always been a strange, mystical box of surprises to me, and I did not want to spoil the gift from Providence. But I have been giving it careful consideration since the events of late." She sighed, then kept on, "I could see the future as an adventure; slowly unfolding, but glorious. Now, I do not know..." She was silent for a minute, and Myra came close to enquiring if she was okay, but then she finished her line of thought, "or rather, I do know, and what I know scares me, leaves me petrified, and shakes me to the core of my being. Still I know that if we endure the hardships ahead and fight until our very last breath, we will conquer. Not the day, but the future, for ourselves and for the coming generations." Myra stood there and let the words sink in; she was overwhelmed and somehow grateful, grateful that there was to be something after this ordeal, at least for those who lived to see the other side of it. Elderanna touched her shoulder lightly, "I cannot say that we will win, there are too many uncertain elements, but I will say that as long as we hold our own and stay together, we stand a chance."

Sadly, Myra nodded and said slowly, "As long as you have hope, Elderanna, then there is hope for us all, even for me...though I will not see it come true..." Elderanna enveloped her in her embrace and after the tears stilled, they walked back to the cabin in silence, carrying the flower leaves in a small basket, covered with a blanket.

Rajan was thoughtful. He was standing on the castle wall, gazing into the night enveloping everything in a soft sheen, while looking inwards into himself. "What am I doing?!?" He was genuinely distressed. He had been training the new recruits in the field outside the town when he saw Myra make her way to Elderanna's cottage. At first only noticing it without thinking, but then he got to marvelling over how fast they had become close, and then...he completely threw himself off guard by thinking, "I wonder what that would be like—being close to Elderanna?" Shocked at his own thought, he did not see the approaching recruit and ended up with a sore jaw and a headache... Well, he got his just desserts! Smiling a little, he decided it was time for bed and made his way past the guards, but he was still thinking about Elderanna...

Chapter 9
The Wayward Wind

The cave lay in complete darkness, a darkness so dense it weighed down on anything and everything present— crushingly. In the middle of the cavern, a seemingly lonely figure stood, undetected by human eyes, but visible to those who could see his body warmth. Not that there was a lot of that, he was clearly a coldblooded creature, but he showed up on the inhabitant's vision, anyway. Or perhaps it was that aura of magic he had, that strong, cold, blue-white shining aura, invisible to the naked eye, but visible to all magical beings and creatures of darkness. Then, there was light. A tiny globe of intense greenish light appeared and grew blindingly fast, soon filling the whole cavern. It was not a pleasant green, like sunlight through leaves would have been. No, it had a venomous, sickly hue to it that mirrored the man who had conjured it: Rhanddemarr. Physically, he did not appear particularly big and strong, though he had a well-knit frame and sinewy muscles, but mentally, that was another thing altogether. When you looked into his slightly bigger than normal eyes, you got a feeling of drowning in them—in deep, dark puddles of murky brown and black, like a tar-pit. And yet they were lit from within, with that same greenish, sick hue that now lay in every corner of the cave, grimly lighting the spectacle that he could see before him.

The surfaces of the enormous cavern were filled with creatures of every conceivable size, shape and hue. The whole gathering was a rainbow-coloured madness, writhing and screeching, clawing and biting, snarling and growling. He smiled to himself—the kind of smile that changed his otherwise pleasant features into a horrid mask. Thus, it came as no surprise when he raised his arms straight up in the air and cried in commanding voice, "Be quiet, my friends, be quiet! You have been patient these long years, but now you shall be patient no longer. Now you will take to the air, swim through the rivers, waters and lakes, and burrow through the ground! You will burst through their barriers like pyroclastic flows and lay their lands barren and empty, and you shall conquer! Your victory is near, your time is at hand, your dominion shall last for a million years to come—for the unforeseeable future! Rise and smell their fear, taunt their feeble attempts at fighting back, eat their courage like sweet berries and spit out despair: You will win the day! Follow me into history!"

A mighty chorus of hissing, snarling, and roaring broke loose like a dam that breaks, and carried on his adoring followers' backs, he entered the dark night under the light of faltering stars. The cold air, coming from the glaciers on the mountain's peaks, greeted them. The icy winds chilled them to the bone, but in their ecstasy, they hardly felt it.

Then a silence fell among them; before their eyes, the wizard was rising slowly and majestically into the air! He stopped just high enough so that all of them could see him, and then he spoke again, clearly, slowly and in measured tones this time, "Our first attack starts immediately. There are persons of interest in their midst, people I greatly wish to see and talk to. Then, there are also the leaders of these people, filthy scum, but strong, nonetheless. They will need a lesson in humility, and we will dole it out to them! Cut the head off the beast and the body will crumple and fall!"

With this, he released the hold he had on them, and troops of various creatures flew, dug, and slithered into the night, all bound by the same purpose, all with determination written in every line of their sneering countenances. They were accompanied by the ever-present wind, and the steady chanting of the wizard, low-keyed and ominous in the background.

The days flew by as they will when there is something to fill them with. When Rajan had returned a few days earlier, looking grave and worried, he had been enclosed with Mojastic for quite a while. Afterwards, when they appeared from Mojastic's chambers, they both looked worn and weary. Myra had seen them as they appeared in the courtyard and had been struck by their identical frowns and harried looks. This morning, when she saw them again together, they were still wearing the same looks on their faces, which made her concerned. She hurried to meet them, and in doing so registered something new in the wind. Stopping, she listened with a puzzled look on her face, "What is that sound? It is almost like someone whistling far, far away, but I can't make it out for sure."

General Rajan saluted her, before he answered, "No one can, but it is always present in Terafuma these days, whistling away at the edge of hearing so that none can be sure if they are actually hearing it or imagining that it is there."

Mojastic looked at them both, "I think it is time we call another meeting of the council, but this time we call in everyone connected to the army as well." Myra and Rajan nodded in agreement, but when Rajan left to see to that it was carried out, Myra asked Mojastic what news Rajan had brought with him. She had a sinking feeling when she thought about it.

Mojastic, absently stroking her hair, turned her around so that he could look her in the eyes. "The news is grave and bewildering," he said, "and it demands more than one wise mind to decipher." Taking her hand, he led her quietly into the castle and down to the council chamber.

In the chamber, servants were making ready for the council meeting. They were setting up chairs, hanging up maps and generally getting the room ready for what was going to be a long day, including water and other refreshments for the council members. When they left, Mojastic and Myra found themselves alone for a minute. They did not speak, but spent the time in silence, enjoying each other's company. After a few minutes Elderanna arrived, closely followed by Grimor, both looking serious and thoughtful. As the rest of the council filtered in, Mojastic took advantage of the respite and called on Grimor's attention, "Could I have a word with you, old friend?" Grimor approached slowly—he did everything slowly these days, Mojastic thought—and sat down with a sigh of contentment. "You look weary; I hope we are not putting too much on your shoulders these days?" Mojastic said, putting his hand on said shoulder.

"No, no, not at all," answered Grimor with a faint smile, "it is just that I seem to be incapable of thinking as fast as I used to. It feels like there is always a sound there disturbing me whenever I start on a train of thought, although when I try to listen, I cannot make it out for sure."

Mojastic clapped him on the shoulder and said, "That is precisely the reason why we are here today; the introduction of a new kind of opposition from our adversary."

He stood up and raised his voice over the din of the assembly, "Hear me, good friends! We are now experiencing the second wave of the opponent's magic: the confusion and confounding stage. It is a situation that closely resembles the first one, with the dreams, but this goes specifically after people in administrative roles; people who need to have a clear mind and focused thoughts. As with the dreams, it seems innocent enough at first, but as it progresses it gets worse and worse and eventually people who are subjected to this torture lose their minds completely!"

The council looked at each other—some in confusion, some in alarm, and some with a dawning realisation in their eyes—and then turned their attention to Mojastic once again. "General Rajan will tell you more about this new challenge, as it has been at work in Terafuma for a while now."

General Rajan then took the centre of the room with all eyes following him. Clearing his throat, he then began to relate his tale, "During my stay in Terafuma I noticed some— oddities, you might say—in people's behaviour. At first, I did not think much of it—after all they had been afflicted with the dreaming and magical disease with more strength than we had—but after some time it started to puzzle me in earnest. At the same time, I also noticed a strange paralysis in their administrative functions, it seemed almost like they were exhausted. When Ingan and Tarlief arrived, I confided in them and they went to work on the problem at once, parallel with their given task of relieving the screaming sickness. It did not take them long to discover the reason for this confounding: A sound on the edge of hearing that was constant and whose effect it was to drive people slowly but surely towards insanity. The ones who had suffered the longest were the eldest, and they were close to collapsing. All this was happening at the same time, and the people afflicted did not think to complain about it, as there were a lot of more 'important' things to take care of. Thanks to our two, good spellcasters, the situation was turned around and the sound—we hope—eradicated for good."

There was a chorus of exclamations of "Good job!" "Yes!", "That's the way to do it!" and so forth, but then Mojastic spoke again, "It has come to my attention that this phenomenon has started also in Arboria, right in our midst, and as you dealt with it in Terafuma, I would call on you to deal with it here also. We cannot have our advisors and administrators walking around unable to think when our enemy is plotting ever more devastating strategies against us!" With nods of consent, Ingan and Tarlief left the chamber to set to work at once.

Mojastic turned to the council again with a look of grim determination on his face. "We must take action to prevent these strategies from being employed," he said. "It is time to leave the defensive thinking aside and take an offensive attitude." The council nodded in agreement, although there was some hesitancy. "I know that the prospect of going to war is a frightening one, but I'm not suggesting an open attack.

I'm proposing that we rather make our defensive measures more offensive and proactive in character." This time the nods and murmurs of agreement were unanimous. He did not have to say anything else, they settled down in groups according to their tasks and went to work on the strategies immediately.

The army officers, of whom there were a fair number present, settled down to the task of determining which tactical means they had ready at hand. The armed forces of Arboria were 2200 men and women, and more could be conscripted if necessary. Combat groups had already been established, and each group of five could be joined together with four other groups to become a unit. Four units then made a division and five divisions made a chamber. In the regular army, each chamber had a general lieutenant. There were four chambers all told, and these were all led by General Rajan. The engineer's corps—one division—were led by General Ordovan, and the navy (or river corps)—also one division strong—were led by General Trecon. The Arborian army had been more than enough through history to handle what little skirmishes there had been, but now their numbers were not up to the task that was before them. The first order of the day for the generals and general lieutenants that were present, was therefore to swell their ranks considerably. This, they did, by conscripting every man and woman over sixteen years of age, and to extend the period of service till the age of sixty. When all those new conscripts had gotten their training and were battle-ready, the army would be increased by eight new chambers, and in addition there would be an extra unit for both the river corps and the engineers.

Obviously, they did not mean for all of these to see active duty, but tasks such as provisions, logistics and administration could be given to those who were not fit for fighting. They all knew the importance of food and shelter in a skirmish or war, and the services these new conscripts could render, could prove priceless. When it came to those who were in prime fighting condition, they would be given as thorough an education as soldier as time allowed, before going out in a fight. The question of time was a source of never-ending worry to them all. But all they could do, was to make ready for whatever was coming their way.

The group that dealt with magical defences were sitting in a closed circle in the back of the room, seemingly oblivious to the exclamations and general buzzing of voices in the room. An observer would have thought they were sleeping—all sitting there with their eyes closed and hardly breathing—but that was far from the case. Their bodies were present, but their minds were in the astral plane, flying above Arboria, to search for any and all signs of untoward activity. This was a dangerous task, as they all knew, for the adversary had proven himself mightier than they liked to think of. But it had to be done, and since Elderanna was the most skilled in using her powers—the others were mere novices as they had never had the need for this in earnest before—she was constantly on watch for any signs of danger, however minute they might be.

As they soared over Arboria, they saw many things that worried them, animals fleeing, rivers seemingly blocked and flooding into the forest on both sides, dying trees and foliage losing its brightness, in some places turning brown and lifeless. It was a sickness of decay, spreading slowly from the northern edge of the land and southwards. There were no clear signs of enemy action, but there were plenty of indicators of foul play. Suddenly, Elderanna became aware of a sound. It sounded a bit like a child singing in that toneless voice that they sometimes use, but at the same time it had a menacing tone to it. The voice was almost unheard to begin with, but it quickly grew in strength until it became a sort of vibration in her skull, hammering at her senses. Overpowered for a minute, she lost her bearings, and it was only the quick reaction of Mojastic that saved her from a sickening fall. He bore her up long enough for her senses to reconnect with reality, and when they did, her response to this attack was swift. A ray of bright, white light shot from her brow into the thickets along the riverbank below and was rewarded with a scream of pain. The ghoul who had been hiding there tried to flee, but to no avail; she followed him with her mind and chased him into the sunlight, where he burned to ashes within the space of seconds. The scene below them then became blurred as the group hurried home to safety.

They all stirred in their chairs and awoke, gasping for air. The group now looked at Elderanna with a deepened respect and even awe. "How did you do that?" Myra asked quietly.

"I don't know," said Elderanna and sat up, slowly as if it hurt her to do so. "It felt like something woke up inside me, something I've never felt before or even knew existed."

"Well, whatever it was, it was just in the nick of time," said Mojastic, but his eyes belied his easy voice. He was studying Elderanna with watchful eyes, and he did not let up for a long time.

The large group of military officers was stunned by the way they had re-animated and were concerned when they learned what had befallen them. They were most interested in what the group had seen during their surveillance of the land but were equally shocked when the findings were laid before them.

"This development is most severe and calls for action," rumbled the voice of Ordovan. As general for the engineers, he was used to dealing with all kinds of natural calamities, and he felt sure they would have something to stem the tide with, so to speak. It was decided that he would take a group of three officers and a unit of soldiers up north to see what could be done with the situation. They would be accompanied by Elderanna, who would keep vigil for any magical traps or assailants.

This was the situation when they broke up to have an hour of rest and refreshment, and they quickly filtered out in the clear air. Only Mojastic stood alone in the council chamber, staring intently at the maps on the walls—the one of Mount Dorth in particular.

When they convened again for the afternoon session, Mojastic greeted them with a strained look on his face. Worrying and apprehensive looks were on all faces as they seated themselves in the room. Mojastic was standing in the middle, like a statue, looking ready to speak, but not uttering any sound—yet. Elderanna was the last person into the room, and when she entered—chatting gaily with Myra—she became abruptly quiet. Exchanging glances with Mojastic, she became very serious and then she approached him with a hurried step. "My Lord," she said anxiously, "are you alright?" He made no response, just stared blankly into the air with a strained expression on his face.

"Everyone, out!" Elderanna suddenly became all business. "Myra, Tarlief, Ingan; join me! We have some serious enchantments to break!" All three of them came forward, almost running, and joined her in front of Mojastic.

"He stayed behind when we recessed for lunch," Myra said. "He said he wanted to think things over in peace and quiet."

Elderanna nodded. "Yes, but he must have done something more than just think...what if he tried to access the site where I was attacked to search for clues?"

Myra gasped, "But that would be exceptionally dangerous! What was he thinking of???"

Ingan and Tarlief were standing there, following the discussion, but not interrupting. Finally, Tarlief asked, "How can we help him?"

Elderanna hesitated for a moment, then ordered them to stand around Mojastic in a close circle with Myra in front of him, holding his hands, and Tarlief and Ingan on each side of him. She herself stood behind him with her hands outstretched over his head. When everyone was in position, she began to speak, "Light, I call upon you! Shine down and lift the shadows that cloud his mind. Light, I implore you: fill this man's being with your rays, fill him up with your warmth, drive all shadows from his being, and alight the fire in his heart! Light, I direct you into this man's soul to fill his being with love and caring!" She lifted her hands up as she spoke, and a ray of white light, stunning in its brightness, shone down, seemingly from nowhere. It enveloped Mojastic in a bright cocoon and obliterated him completely. Myra, who was holding his hands, had the impression of her hands vanishing into a white nothingness. But then, he began to re-emerge from the cocoon as the light slowly withdrew to wherever it came from. Anxiously, they looked into his eyes. He blinked slowly, and then reason and understanding suddenly appeared in his eyes again. He looked terrified for a split second, and then he relaxed visibly.

Sighing with relief, Tarlief and Ingan walked on shaky legs over to the table in the middle, found two chairs and sat down. Myra knelt in front of Mojastic who had sat down in an armchair by the wall. Looking intently into his eyes, she asked him, "How are you? What happened?"

He looked sadly and somewhat shameful at her, and then he shook his head, "I was overconfident and worried at the same time. Not a good combination for any kind of decision process, and especially not when you decide to do magical surveillance on your own, which was what I did."

At this, Elderanna's eyes narrowed, and she got ready for a real scolding, but he intercepted her, "I know! It was stupid of me, stupid and idiotic beyond measure, and I know that I was incredibly lucky and fortunate to have such good and skilled helpers. You literally saved my skin."

They looked at him questioningly. "What happened, and what did you meet?" Elderanna asked quietly, but sternly.

"I met a shapeshifter and a soul-sucker," he answered, "and they combined to take me down. Now they did not manage to do that, but I was frozen by their spells which intertwined to capture me. All I could do was to hang motionless in the air, while something was approaching from behind. Something darker and more terrible than either, and it was coming for me, for my soul."

Elderanna hid her face in her hands for a moment before looking up again. Looking into his eyes for a second, she smiled and then she stood up, "It all ended well, despite the foolishness of one of our number…hrmf! Now we had better get the rest of the council back in here, before they start to call in the guards, or the army for that matter!" Although she was making light of the experience, they had just been through, it was clear that she was both worried and extremely relieved.

When the rest of the council re-entered the chamber, they all wore expressions of worry or anxiety on their faces, but that look was replaced by relief as Elderanna related what had happened and that all had ended, if not satisfactorily, then at least well. They settled back to business again and as the hours flew by, the graveness of the whole situation settled on their shoulders like a gigantic leech, sucking the life and spirits out of them until they could take it no more.

"Enough!" said Mojastic in his strong voice. "We need sleep, all of us, and especially those that will be going on the expedition to the north tomorrow. You have some preparing to do if I am not mistaken?"

General Ordovan nodded, then spoke, "We have something to inform you of," he said. "In addition to myself and the soldiers, General Rajan will be accompanying us as guard for Elderanna. It seems that this force that we are up against has something against witches and wizards, and so it could be wise to have an extra pair of eyes and a capable hand, just in case."

Mojastic nodded, secretly relieved, "Thank you Ordovan, and a special thank you to Rajan. The offer is gratefully accepted." With that, the council withdrew and stepped out into the fragrant night on their way to their quarters. As Elderanna walked to her cottage, she was joined by a shadow. General Rajan stepped up beside her and together they walked in silence—both very tired, but also enjoying the quiet night surrounding them. In front of her cottage entrance, he saluted her with a smile on his lips and then walked briskly back to his own rooms.

The next day dawned as beautiful, warm and inspiring as the last, and it was with some excitement that Elderanna set about preparing what little she would need on their foray to the north. Yes, she was apprehensive about what awaited them there, but she was also looking forward to the trip through lush, green woodland and dancing brooks. A knock on the doorframe made her turn around. General Rajan was standing there, framed by the doorway, and smiling at her, "Can I be of service to you?" he asked.

Elderanna smiled back, it was simply impossible to resist, and answered, "Yes, in fact you can! Could you take this bundle of mine down to the exercise yard where we agreed to meet?" Giving her a small salute, he picked up the bundle, indeed very small, and retreated from the door.

She picked out a few more of her remedies and put them in a sling that she was carrying, and then she joined him on the outside. "What a gorgeous day!" she exclaimed as they started walking. He smiled again, this time broadly; her girlish enthusiasm was infectious.

"Indeed, it is," he answered, and walked on with a spring in his step.

When they met up with the rest of the group, they first made sure that everything they would or could possibly need, had been packed into the backpacks that the soldiers were carrying. The officers, Theyn, Argil, and Benach, also had backpacks to carry, as well as the generals. The only person not carrying a backpack was Elderanna, but as she was going to be their magical scout, she already carried a heavy burden and did not need to be cumbered with a physical load as well.

Just as they passed out of the gates, they spotted a man on horseback. When he came nearer, they recognised Mojastic. *He looked dashing seated high up on horseback with the sun in his back, like a character from the old myths*, Elderanna thought to herself. As they approached one another, he leaped off the saddle with ease and walked toward them, reins held loosely in his hand. "I wanted to see you off," he said, "and wish you a safe expedition and a speedy return."

"Thank you, sire, that is most kind of you," said Rajan as he shook hands with the king. "Now, let us get going. The world does not stop for us or anyone else, and time is wasting!" With that, they were off, and the last Mojastic saw of them, was them disappearing into a golden haze on the top of the hill.

Mojastic's thoughts were clouded with uneasiness as he sat in the throne room. The large room was cool and inviting, its shadows soft and soothing and its curtains just shady enough to give comfort without blocking the view. Still, he had dark thoughts. He worried about the task force currently on their way to the northern forest, he worried over Myra's silence these last days, was she not well? And on top of that there were the nagging doubts he had about Arcull. True, the man had common sense, was a trustworthy advisor, had an excellent knowledge of people and geography, and was a loyal servant. The problem was, who was he loyal to? Where did his allegiance lie? He sighed. These were dire questions and he knew he had to find the answer to them before they were hurt by them, but how was he to lure the truth out of Arcull and who could he possibly ask for information without sending him a warning?

Chapter 10
The Missing

Myra had kept herself to the background while these proceedings went on. She felt a little in the way and tried to keep a low profile for the time being. Although a queen, and a strong one at that, she was unfamiliar with the rituals and set ways of the people of Arboria. Also, she did not want to make any disturbances while these deliberations lasted; there was too much at stake. Now, however, she enjoyed the respite in the aftermath of the preparations, and though she knew that the waiting period to come would feel like an age, she basked in the sun, letting her mind run free—for a moment, at least.

Mojastic, having taken another ride to clear his mind, stood at the entrance to the private garden and looked at her. He had this feeling inside, like his heart was too big for his body and somehow wanted to break free. How was it even possible to love someone so totally, absorbingly after only a day's acquaintance??? He did not expect to get an answer to this question, and only gazed at her where she lay and thrilled at the sight.

Becoming aware of his glances, Myra sat up abruptly, then relaxed and smiled. It was a smile that lit up her face from within, the sort of smile that stays with you forever, long after the person whom the smile belonged to has ceased to exist. She waved Mojastic over and bid him lie down on the lawn with her. Lying on his back, looking up at her beautiful countenance, he thought to himself, *This is what they mean by 'paradise'.* And then, when she leant over him and kissed him, his mind and thoughts were gone like fluttering butterflies in a summer field.

The company that was headed northwards, made satisfactory progress. They marched forward through woods and glens, following a small brook that kept dwindling as they crept slowly up in the highlands to the north. Elderanna was constantly on the watch for any foes from within or without, but so far nothing had presented itself to her. Not that she expected it to, at least not before nightfall. She noticed the woods changing character, becoming darker and less penetrable, but so far that was more a feeling than reality. *Probably our expectations colouring our observations,* she thought, then shook her head. *No use worrying about what might come, it will present itself soon enough.* With that, she closed her internal monologue and returned to observing the surroundings, mentally and physically. As they neared the top of the ridge, they came to a small clearing, all strewn with pine needles, creating a soft carpet beneath their feet. Their muffled footprints sounded eerie, but when they reached the far side of the clearing, they found some fallen trees, old by the sight of them and of good size. That was where they decided to make a halt and have something to eat and drink, before continuing their journey.

Half an hour went by, with near no sound at all, except the sounds of munching and drinking. They were not tired—the walk had so far not been strenuous—but they all seemed downhearted and dispirited. Mulling these matters over in her mind, Elderanna suddenly noticed a strange movement in the carpet of needles. She jumped up and—quick as a lightning flash—threw out a spell. The monstrous creature that was rising from the needle carpet looked like a grotesque crossbreed of a huge porcupine and a wolverine, with an extra set of sharp teeth. It was quick as well, almost escaping the force of her spell, but not quite. With the sound of a large splash, it exploded over the clearing, scattering smoking, wet pieces over the surroundings as well as over the shocked spectators. Stunned, Rajan turned to see if Elderanna was unharmed. To his dismay and horror, she was gone! Only her bag remained where she had stood only seconds ago! Panic quickly rose within him, but he fought it down and started a search with the rest of the group. They all spread out in a familiar and well-rehearsed pattern, but never further apart than they could glimpse the others through the branches. Where was she??? How could she have disappeared so completely in such a short time??? They called and searched, but to no avail.

Elderanna was flying, soaring high up above them, looking down on their confusion. She was astounded by what had happened, but not afraid; it felt natural, like she had always known how to accomplish this...

'Elaidar' came to mind 'bird of prey' in a tongue she did not know and yet knew. While hanging in the air, she could see for miles upon end, and she surveyed the landscape with a keen eye. Due north, she could see dark shadows inside the forest, moving southwards, towards the company. In a heartbeat she was back on the ground among the group, now nearly franticly searching behind and under every bush. The sudden appearance of Elderanna sent them diving for cover, before, equally fast, they were up and rejoicing over her return. Rajan looked totally flabbergasted but managed to pull himself together when she broke off their chattering with, "They are coming this way as we speak; dark shadows moving from the north! And I'll explain it all after we have overcome them." Now, everyone knew what they were expected to do and set about to get prepared for the attack. They all went into hiding in the trees and bushes, except Rajan, Ordovan and Elderanna. These three remained on the ground and waited silently for the enemy.

They could hear the attackers before they saw them, the slithering sounds of something slimy and scaly moving along the forest floor. To this sound was added the panting and wheezing of laborious breath and a hissing noise that they quickly identified as the creatures' voices, harsh and snake-like. As they awaited the attack, Elderanna tried to identify the creatures from the sound and what little she had seen of them. She was struggling with this; the only picture that came to mind was the common garden snake in her own backyard, but that could not be it. Then it hit her, Daemoins! With the revelation came the insight, "We must regroup, fast!" She caught hold of the two men standing next to her and whispered hurriedly into their ears. They both reacted as if stung, and got their men moving to new positions as fast as humanly possible. Still, it was barely in time, for they had not even caught their breath when the attack started.

There were four of them: giant, scaly monsters. Terrifying to look at, even worse to hear, for their voices were constantly hissing, squealing and rasping like a thousand insects on rusty metal. The hissing also meant that they were spitting and spraying venom around as they rushed towards the three humans on the ground. Some of this poison inevitably found its way in their faces where it burnt like fire. The men still fought desperately, and due to the accuracy of their arrows, the four serpent-demons were quickly blinded. After that, it was merely a question of who was brave enough to confront the creatures, avoid the tail when they twisted around, and give them the lethal blow with the sword or axe. Many of those present were shakily trying to do this, but General Rajan excelled with his swordsmanship and took down three of the Daemoins alone. Because of Elderanna's foresight and revelation, the soldiers were to some extent prepared for the ordeal, and therefore they did not lose any of the men, but they had a fair number of wounds when the fighting ended.

It was well into the night when they had finished with the disposal of the carcasses. Elderanna insisted on this job, saying that it would confuse the enemy if they just disappeared instead of his scouts finding them hacked to pieces. The clean-up crew consisted of ten soldiers, the three officers and Elderanna. When this job was done, they saw to it that the perimeter of their camp was safe, and then they came back to the others. Five of the soldiers were wounded, but none seriously, and Elderanna now saw to them, washed their wounds, gave them something for the pain they were in, and left them relieved. However, when she spoke, it was with seriousness in her voice, "Gentlemen, this was a close call, too close for comfort! Even though we were walking with care, taking every precaution that we could imagine, it still was not enough."

"No, but thanks to you, we still saved the day, even if it hung in the balance for a while," said Rajan.

Ordovan nodded, then added, "I would dearly like to know what happened just before the attack. Where were you and how did you know they were on their way?"

Elderanna smiled at his quizzical face, "I was elaidaring, that is, 'flying invisible like a bird of prey,' and before you ask, no, I had no idea that I could do it, none at all."

"So, basically, you went sinestraling, but this time with your body?" Rajan asked, looking genuinely interested.

"Yes" Elderanna said, "And not only that, I could see much wider and clearer than I have ever been able to do with the sinestral." They stood there for a while, discussing the events of the day, but then they decided it was time for some rest and went quietly to their blankets under a clear field of stars. *Oh, the beauty of the naked night sky!* Elderanna thought just before slipping off to her waking sleep—on guard as always.

In the castle, Myra woke with a chill running down her back. What was that sound that had woken her? She got quietly out of the big bed she shared with Mojastic, so as not to disturb his sleep, but to no avail. He woke up the moment she left his side and sat up in bed, "What is the matter?" he asked, looking keenly at her eyes.

"I heard a noise," she said, "and wanted to find out what it was. It gave me a cold chill down my back, but now I can't hear anything."

"Could it be the whistling curse?" Mojastic asked.

"No," she answered, "Ingan and Tarlief were adept at stopping that. This is something else, something darker or more dangerous." While she was talking, she became aware of the sound again, now nearer.

Mojastic heard it too and jumped out of bed, "Myra, hurry! Get away from the window!" He jumped forward and just managed to tear her away before a great foot with long, sharp talons came in through the windowpane. It just barely missed her as it swiped from left to right and then withdrew. Mojastic was on his feet, bellowing on the top of his lungs for his guards, and drawing his sword from the scabbard on the wall as he did this. Keeping Myra safely behind his back, he turned his attention back to the window again, and what he saw rocked his senses. It looked like a flying snake, with huge eagle's wings and a troll's head, an abomination of a sick mind. It had two legs, like an eagle, with long, sharp, and possibly even venomous talons—there was some sort of liquid dripping from them at any rate—and its mouth was filled with jagged and uneven teeth, made for crushing bone and rendering flesh. A horrendous spectacle made for haunting a madman's dreams. When it spotted him looking at it, it screeched and threw itself at the castle wall, clearly mad with rage. Arrows came whistling from beneath, a whole cloud of them, piercing the creature's wings, eyes and body. As it fell to the ground with a huge, bone crunching 'thud', it became silent. Only a tiny wailing came from the creature's mouth as it breathed its last breath.

"Oh, Mother, what was that creature?" asked Myra with a quavering voice. She was shocked at the speed with which the creature had attacked, and at how unprepared she had been. She had not been able to defend herself, even though she was more than adept at using her magical powers.

Mojastic was none too steady either, when he replied, "I have absolutely no idea, but we will find out!" He held her steady with an arm around her shoulders, keeping her warm in the night that suddenly seemed cold.

In his abode deep within Mount Dorth, Rhanddemarr was fuming. His first attacks had been subtle and not easily detected, yet somehow, they had been thwarted. And now, two attacks in two different locations and with different approaches had been struck down! He knew that Elderanna had been part of that scouting troop in the north, but he was unable to see how the beasts had been defeated. And the last one...who was the culprit there? Who was strong enough to keep his magnificent beast at bay while the archers did their part??? He closed his fist tightly and swore under his breath, "You will pay for this, all of you!"

Chapter 11
A King's Son

As the summer progressed, it became evident that the union between Mojastic and Myra was a fruitful one. Not only in their capacities as king and queen of their respective countries, but also on a personal level. In their official capacity, they were now cooperating massively, bringing the armies of both countries together and coordinating their efforts. With both armies being strengthened by hordes of conscripts and volunteers, they could now defend their borders much more efficiently than before. Also, the newfound cooperation between the countries had ripple-effects down into the populations of both, the people were talking together, working together, and coming up with innovative ideas and schemes to help the situation. It was in truth a union in the making.

On the personal level, the two monarchs proved to fulfil each other commendably, with their strengths and weaknesses balancing out harmoniously. They were like Siamese twins, and yet two distinct rulers with their own personal style and way of doing things. With all the hubbub and clamour of increasing activity at the borders, and more and more frequent attacks of various kinds, they were two towers, side by side, standing calmly in the storm.

Elderanna was concerned, nonetheless. She knew—as one of very few—that there was another thing growing in this relationship. Day by day she watched Myra's body changing in subtle ways, to accommodate the new life she was getting ready to bring to the world. She was not showing much, it was more a question of little things she did, like, taking fewer risks, eating more regularly, sleeping more, smiling more, being more fluid in her movements—all of them signs of pregnancy in a gaiatleran female, but not readily recognised by the people of Arboria.

But soon enough the rumours started spreading from mouth to mouth and then in the marketplaces. The Queen was with child, the King was going to be a father, and all that they had wished for was going to happen! As midsummer was approaching, the king decided it was time for a public announcement, and with the queen by his side, he stood proudly in front of the council and told them of the impending birth. When the cheers and clapping were beginning to die out, Methena asked if it was his plan to announce this to the public at large as well, and when he confirmed this, they all started planning how and when this should be done.

Elderanna did not partake in this discussion. She was standing, half in shadow, beside a large cabinet in the back of the council chamber, looking thoughtful and serious. Rajan approached her, a little cautiously, as if he was afraid of disturbing her train of thought. But when he came close to her, he found her with a little mischievous grin on her face. "Hmmm, sneaking around like the proverbial pussycat! What might you be up to?"

Rajan blushed before he answered, "Well, with you standing here with that countenance, I thought I should best approach you with caution lest you incinerate me for attacking you!"

"My, oh my, what a reputation I have grown!" laughed Elderanna. "Is everyone as afraid of me, or is it just you?" Before he could reply, a shrill bell sounded through the castle walls, and cries and thumping sounds were heard emanating from the courtyard. Without any ado, he was out of the door, quicker than lightning.

Up in the courtyard he was met with a scene of complete havoc, building stones, mortar, and logs from the building structures were lying strewn about like debris after a flood. The kitchens had partially collapsed and the cries from wounded people inside were heart breaking to listen to. With a glance around the yard, he got an overview of the situation, and it did not please him. Amid the cries of the wounded, the sounds of falling debris from the building, and the calls from emergency nurses and other people, doing the best they could to help, he heard a low-pitched, throaty growl that he could not immediately place.

Puzzled, he stood there for a split second, but that was all it took for the source of the sound to reveal itself. A huge lizard-like creature, with scaly brown-speckled skin, eyes with heavy lids that closed like a snake's, and a mouth full of row upon row of sharp, lethal-looking teeth stared straight at him with a venomous look in its eyes. A chill ran down his spine, but he stood there, outwardly calm, and waited for the beast to make its move.

It did, with blinding speed. It struck straight at the place where he stood and had not Elderanna been in the courtyard at that moment, the story of Rajan's life would have ended right there and then. Elderanna, however, was present, running up the stairs as fast as was possible. Even on the way over the threshold, she had her spells ready to be cast, and without any delay her voice rang out loudly, above the noise surrounding her. The beast reacted as if it had been hit and snarled in defiance. It tried to attack Elderanna, but her voice, or her words were slowing it down, and when the soldiers present struck at it with the weapons, they had available, they managed to pin it down and kill it, although it took some time before the beast gave up its breath.

Rajan, although not killed, had been hurt by the beast, and was lying prostrate on the ground, not making a sound. Elderanna ran to his side and knelt breathlessly next to him. Quickly she checked his breathing, his colour and his joints and bones to see if anything was broken or damaged, but when she could not find anything, she started calling for him in a commanding voice. After what seemed like an age, he responded with a grunt, and Elderanna visibly relaxed. "This time you scared me," she whispered.

Rajan opened one eye and looked at her slyly, "Hmmm? What was that? Not an admission of affection, eh?" Elderanna got up so quickly, she dropped his head which she'd cradled in her lap, "Pah, you are delusional," she said, and hurried away, but not without a last glance over her shoulder, and—he could have sworn—a wink!

When the dust settled, and the casualties were counted, they realised that they had been lucky. Only fourteen dead, despite the caving in of the kitchens, and thirty or so wounded. Rajan himself had been winded by the impact of the attack, and three of his ribs were bruised, but otherwise he was completely unharmed, thanks to Elderanna. *People were milling about in the market place, in the town square, and in the streets, all of them acting like beheaded chickens*, Myra thought. When exchanging glances with Mojastic, she could tell he was thinking along the same lines.

Sighing, he lifted up his voice and called for their attention, "People of Arboria, be at peace! The beast has been vanquished and the hurt are being cared for. My thoughts are with those of us who have lost a dear one; we all grieve with you and stand with you in your sorrow! Now, we must act, so the council are called into session immediately. Soldiers will be put on patrol in the near vicinity of the town, and nurses will visit all the houses to see to it that every need is met as far as we can make it."

With those words, he left the gateway to the courtyard and made his way into the interior of the castle again. The council followed him slowly back to the chamber.

Another a few weeks went by, and life returned to almost normal pace again. They went about their summerly chores and kept the farms and the animals as tidy and well as they could, but underneath lay an anxiety that was impossible to overlook, the anxiety of another attack, or perhaps a new kind of attack. That little nervousness that hurried people's steps when they were going from the house to the barn or back, or hurrying home late at night, after the shops were closed. To set people's minds at ease, Mojastic and Myra decided it was time for the announcement of the upcoming birth of the royal heir.

Standing together, hand in hand in the town square, they announced the coming birth of their firstborn, and the applause from the people gathered there, told them everything they needed and wanted to know. People were openly crying, cheering, hugging each other, and were generally exuberant. Smiling, the royal couple waved at everyone and then walked back into the castle, still holding hands.

When the time came for the royal birth, the summer was full, and the harvest was almost ripe. Attacks were frequent by now, and the death tolls were rising, but even so the people of the two kingdoms managed to rejoice and make merry. When the queen went into labour late in the evening, almost everyone thought that the baby would be a short time in coming. As it worked out, it took more time than expected, and by noon the next day, people were beginning to look worried.

Myra was not lying in bed; she was pacing the floor, impatiently, while waves of labour pains racked her body. She would not lie down, that was not the custom of her people, but she gratefully accepted the water Mojastic held out for her. He was also allowed to wash her head and back gently with a wet, cold sponge to ease her pains.

Finally, when the sun set, the birth itself began, and then the pace picked up. With the flaming sunset as backdrop, the new royal prince—Myrathion I—was introduced to the people below, cheering wildly when Mojastic held him high up in the air to greet his future subjects. Myra, standing in the bedchamber, smiled gently at the sight, but underneath the smile lay a grimace of pain, deeper and more agonising than anyone could guess at. Elderanna, standing in the courtyard with the crowd, could only glimpse Myra, but what she saw frightened her. *She is already fading!* Elderanna thought. *All too soon, all too soon. Oh, what ordeals lie in wait for him now!* Wiping tears from her eyes, she walked slowly out of the castle grounds and made her way home, walking slowly.

Chapter 12
Red Sunset Dark Dawn

As the sun set in a sea of flaming reds, a calm silence descended on the town. People were out, enjoying the last rays of sunshine before going inside for their evening meal and rest. It was a quiet night, a night for contemplation, for lovers, and for family. Rajan was sitting alone on a bench in the gardens, just smelling the fragrant air. It was bliss, sitting like this in the fading light of day, in between confrontations and strife. He was tired, dead tired, worn out by battles and skirmishes along the borders almost every day. Still, he was not one to give up and lie down, so he tried to pull his tired limbs into action.

Just as he succeeded in bringing his body to an upright position, he sensed someone in the garden with him. He strained his eyes to see into the shade under the bahliama trees, but the shadows in there were so dense, it was impossible to see anything. Slowly, the outline of a figure, darker than the rest of the shadows, materialised in front of his eyes. Gliding—ever so slowly—towards him, he was part curious and part sceptical of this creature, whatever it was.

His sixth sense suddenly sent out an alarm that shook his whole body, but by then it was too late. The creature suddenly seemed to speed up its approach and then he found himself face to face with something so cold that it sent his body into shivers and drove his mind blank with fear. Pure darkness it was, pure darkness and a lust for his soul, strength and mind, in that order. He felt himself crumple up, shrivelling like a grape in the sun, except it was darkness that was claiming him. He was defenceless, unable to move or even scream, although in his mind he cried out to the one he was most sorry for disappointing.

And his cries were heard. In a flash she was there, shooting bolts of light into the darkness, forcing it to withdraw—hissing and spitting, baring its fangs. Rajan's legs gave way and he dropped to his knees on the grass, gasping for air, knowing how close he had come to surrendering.

Meanwhile, Elderanna was forcing the creature to retreat further and further, always keeping it in her light, never letting up for a second, as she knew that the counterattack would be swift if it was given even a moment to catch its footing. At last, she had it cornered up against the castle wall, and with one final bolt—the largest and heaviest she could produce—she burnt it into oblivion. Turning around, she spotted Rajan on his knees, but as she watched, he keeled over on his side. Quickly, she ran and knelt by his side while conjuring up all healing spells she knew.

She looked anxiously into his eyes—dark, dreamy, but full of dread, and tried to read his mind in them. After a long period, he shuddered and closed his eyes and Elderanna relaxed; there was no evil in him and no trace of the other's presence. "Thank the light!" she muttered. "If the attack of the Greitsch was a close call, then I refuse to consider what this was! You are too trusting, my friend, far too trusting. A strange, but wonderful, trait in a soldier."

As she sat there, with the now sleeping Rajan's head in her lap, she allowed herself a game of, 'What if...?' but she quickly called it off, though nice, now was really not the time for such things! Upon studying his face, she noticed how prominent his worry-lines had become and how haggard his appearance was. "You look like you could need a month of sleep," she said with a warm tone in her voice, "we all do."

Sitting on the fragrant grass, the warm night, the stars that had come out in the sky, his soft breathing—she would never know what made her do it, but suddenly she leaned over him and kissed him softly on the mouth. His eyes flew open, startled, and then he wrapped his arms around her and returned the kiss. Lost in the moment, they sought each other's company and physical companionship, and it was not until they had to break the kiss to catch their breath, that they realised what they had been doing.

Blushing, Elderanna tried to free herself, but failed miserably. Whether on account of his strength or because she really did not want to leave, she did not know, nor think more about. Looking up at her were the startling blue-grey eyes of Rajan, now with stars in them—a soft sheen of sparkling lights that illuminated his very soul. Elderanna's eyes were mirroring his, but they were even deeper and showed, even though the stars were behind her, a myriad of stars in their depths. Mesmerised, Rajan pulled her slowly closer until their lips met again, and then the world swirled away.

When they woke up, it was the middle of the night and the moon was due to rise. Looking at the mountaintops to the east, Rajan noticed that something was off. There shone a sickly light below the horizon—a silver-red hue that was all wrong—and then the blood moon made its appearance. "Look!" he said to Elderanna, "a blood moon, and so big! I have never seen it like this before!"

Elderanna gazed solemnly at the moon, then she sighed, "Rajan, I believe we are in for a storm. We had better get to the castle before it breaks!" Getting up quickly, they looked at each other, then exchanged one last kiss before making their way hurriedly toward the castle.

Inside the castle everything was quiet, but not for long. Using the club that was standing by the front door, Elderanna struck the huge gong that was suspended from the roof in the entrance hall, sending deep reverberations throughout the building and waking everyone. As Mojastic appeared, looking worried and quizzical, she quickly explained what she and Rajan had seen and experienced that evening. Looking hard at Rajan, then at Elderanna, Mojastic turned away with a little smile on his lips, but then he became efficiency itself, ordering all to their places and the council to assemble in the throne room. Myra—who had joined them by now—was looking from one to the other, smiling. She made no attempt to hide her smile either, but it was not a mocking smile; she was genuinely happy, although surprised, very surprised indeed.

As the hours went by, the blood moon intensified in colour and luminosity. It was as if it was bringing in a verdict, a death sentence. People were scared and getting more and more terrified as the clock ticked its way toward morning. Threatening storm clouds were gathering in the north, filling the whole horizon from east to west, and slowly menacingly creeping towards the now sinking moon. The

121

moon lit these clouds from below, as it seemed, which made them look even more sinister.

In the end, morning came but it was not the relief they had counted on. The heavy clouds now covered the sky completely with a dark canopy that seemed to hang down the mountains' sides. The morning was dark, darker than in a solar eclipse, almost as dark as the night. Only a faint shimmer was detectable in the air, and that was how they knew that morning was near, but as of yet there was no sunrise and no way to tell the time.

Rajan and Elderanna were talking together in low whispers in a corner of the throne room. The reason for them doing so was relatively obvious; the room, or hall, was filled to the brink with nervous, scared or terrified citizens, trying their best to not panic. Panic was, however, exactly what would have been if they could have heard what was being discussed in the corner.

"It was a Noctemar," Elderanna whispered, "a soul leecher."

"Soul leecher?" Rajan asked, puzzled.

"A being of the dark," she answered, "one that sucks your memories, your life force, your very soul, right out of you and leaves only an empty shell."

His eyes widening in shock, he asked, "But, why? Why me, and why now? It has never before been seen in these parts, so where did it come from? Where does it live? And how did you kill it? Can we do the same?"

Smiling a little, Elderanna put her slender hands on his broad shoulders, "Calm down, dear. All your questions will be answered presently. I am only glad that I got there in time. I shudder to think of the alternative…" Looking deep into each other's eyes, they both found what they had been searching for.

It was Mojastic that broke the spell, "We convene a meeting in the war chamber in ten minutes," he said.

In the war chamber, as the council chamber had been renamed, they all stood quietly while Elderanna recounted the events of the evening and night. She ended her tale just as dawn set in, but when they entered the courtyard above, there was no change to the light.

"No sunrise…" Porlene said in a small voice.

"No sunrise, no sunlight, no light at all!" replied Tarlief, shuddering as he uttered the words. They stood in a semicircle, silent and downcast. The world seemed a strange place, suddenly all that was familiar had been changed, had been distorted into an unsettling image of itself.

"Now the war has truly begun, not only in Arboria, Afamia, and Terafuma, but all over the world of Dragora!" Myra said what everyone was thinking. Slowly, they turned their backs to the dark skies and headed back inside the castle.

Chapter 13
The Beginning of the End

In the silence of the war chamber only the soft sound of crying could be heard—tears spilling down the cheeks of their weary faces—all tired beyond anything they had experienced before. Yet this was only a foreboding of what was to come. For two months now, they had had skirmishes and attacks along the borders, but this was a step up; the adversary had turned up the heat, so to speak, several notches. Such was their grief and despair at that time that they did not at first react to the clanging of bells and sounding of gongs. Rajan—however—was on his feet and on his way out through the door, even before Mojastic had called them to action. "Alarm!" he shouted, "the alarms are sounding! All to their posts!"

When they entered their posts, they could at first not believe what they saw, billowing clouds of dark smoke was building up in the north, looking thunderous and menacing, and sparks were raining from these clouds like droplets, putting their marks on the ground and starting small fires wherever they took hold. These fires were nearing the borders of Arboria and the arid, coarse smell of them filled their noses and made the children retch and cry. Elderanna, Tarlief, and Ingan were soon busy trying to prevent the winds from blowing in their direction—with some success—but one spellcaster was missing. "Myra!" Elderanna suddenly thought. "Where is Myra??? She could be most helpful now with her weather magic!"

As if called for, Myra suddenly stood on the platform of the top tower as she had done before, lifting her arms to the sky and chanting an ancient magic to the clouds. Like the first time she did this, shield lines started to spread outward, following the ancient ley-lines covering the landscape, and wrapping Arboria in a blanket of light, warm and protected. While doing this Myra slowly lifted off from the high platform where she stood, carried on delicate—almost invisible—wings. Letting the magic flow through her, Myra was re-charging the shield she had made for them. Or, that was what she was trying to do. But this time, something was different.

Elderanna, sensing something in her voice, turned to look at her, and what she saw alarmed her greatly. Myra was swaying from side to side, looking almost as if she was in a trance, and a light was spreading outwards from her, growing at an astonishing rate. It grew in intensity until it hurt to look at her directly, and then it exploded like a million-star fires all at once, spreading in all directions and engulfing the spectators in a burst of unconditional love—so strong it made tears well from their eyes and their hearts come close to a standstill. It was an all-powerful moment, and when the aftershock cleared and their eyesight were beginning to be restored, they were all ready to cheer. But what they beheld was a wisp of light slowly falling towards the floor, and a dead silence ensued.

Elderanna was running up the stairs to the tower, faster than she could remember ever having run before, but she had a terrible feeling that it was too late. When she reached the top of the tower, she found Mojastic already there, and the sight of him made her stop at the landing. She watched him kneel with tears flowing down his face as he went to pick up the frail figure lying on the floor. Myra, always slender-bodied, was now merely a ghost—literally. She still shone clearly, though faintly, but she looked translucent, and Elderanna thought she could see the slabs and tiles through the outline of her body. Mojastic was crying silently and Elderanna heard him repeat again and again, "It is too soon…" but in that hour, Myra left the world behind her and vanished into the faint sunlight shining through the clouds for a brief time.

Stunned, unable to believe what she had just witnessed, Elderanna found herself unwilling or unable to move, and she was still standing there when Rajan arrived. He had been with the soldiers by the gate and had not been aware of this incident before it reached its climax. Almost running into Elderanna, he came to an abrupt halt as well, and then he just stood there with his arms around her, trying to console them both—her and himself—but feeling miserably like a failure. Time seemed to stand still, and it was as if the entire world and its inhabitants held their breath, wishing that someone would do something to make the last minutes be undone, somehow. But in the end, Mojastic stood up and righted his back, then turned to walk to the parapet and face the people waiting anxiously down in the courtyard.

When he looked down upon his subjects it was easy to see his grief; it was written in every line of his face, in his posture, and in his eyes—a grief so strong and fresh it tore their hearts out. He lifted his hand up for everyone to see what remained of his beloved Myra, a wisp of silk, the nightgown she had been wearing when they went to sleep that evening. When he started to speak, his voice broke and he had to start over again, "My queen is gone... She went into the light and took my heart with her. And although she went willingly, I know she did not do it gladly, because she left so much behind her here that is, now, out of her grasp... But let not her sacrifice be for nothing! She has given us a moment of respite and set the standard for this battle, and I for one, intend to see it through!" The people, having stood with their heads bowed during his speech, now looked up again and applauded him warmly. It was an applause that said so much more than words could ever do; it spoke of the love they bore for their monarchs, and the sympathy and resolve they shared. Elderanna was crying openly, and Rajan could not hide his tears either. When Mojastic approached the landing to start his heavy descent, they greeted him as old friends and stood there, just embracing each other, for as long a time as the situation allowed.

However, as they stood there, dark clouds were gathering once more, and the skies grew black, tinted with red. A wind picked up, spreading the stench of fire and burning woods. They realised that the fire was coming towards them and hurried down from the castle roof.

Myra's efforts had gained them a much-needed pause in the ongoing battle, but the flames soon caught hold again and threatened to wash over the town if they did not do something quickly. The people were stunned by the fresh grief and bewildered by the situation. They did not know where to turn, and the lack of visibility made it even more difficult for them.

In the north, the thick, dark smoke was billowing over the hills and into the valleys, obscuring their vision and making it even harder to breathe. This made the people standing in the courtyard and outside in the village, break out in a panic. Rajan was soon in the thick of things, ordering evacuation and restoring some measure of rationality in the chaos that had followed in the wake of Myra's demise.

Elderanna felt momentarily at a loss. Standing in the middle of the panic-stricken crowd, she felt for a second like she was going to panic herself. Some people were screaming, sobbing and whimpering, whilst others were cursing and swearing, or just bellowing out their anger and bewilderment. In the middle of this mayhem she suddenly spotted a small group of children—two to seven years old—who were in danger of being trampled in the throng, lost and fearful as they were.

Acting immediately, she went quickly over to the group, and squatting down beside them, protected them with her body while trying to calm them with soothing words and a mild voice. Fortunately, they responded quickly to her efforts, and within a few minutes they were calm enough to be passed on to a group of soldiers who let the children ride in a cart to get them out of harm's way. Mojastic ran into the castle before returning moments later with a bundle wrapped firmly and securely in his arms. The little prince slept, cradled in his father's strong arms without knowing anything of the loss he had just experienced.

In a somewhat organised caravan, the people started to evacuate the village. As they hurried past Elderanna's cottage, she gave it one long, last glance. She felt a pang of sorrow, it had been her home for many years—she could not tell how many—and now it was going to be the prey of the flames…if she could not protect it… In a flurry, she raised her hands and laid an incantation over the cottage and grounds surrounding it. Having done what she could, she allowed herself to be swept along by the tide of people. Everyone in the huddled mass of refugees were in the same boat, they all had to leave their homes and belongings behind them, and the sounds of fresh grief and shock were easy to hear as people uprooted themselves and fled. The military was keeping things ordered and controlled, but many of their soldiers were, of course, engaged in battle elsewhere and could not possibly know of the horrors that had been unleashed here.

As they turned a bend in the road and the village was lost behind them, the flames caught hold in the woods above the castle and soon the mountainside was ablaze, flame-tongues hanging threateningly over the castle walls and engulfing the gardens. Crossing the bridge over the river Arrca they all felt calmer; they were out of reach of the flames—at least for the present. Now they may have escaped the immediate danger, but a new one was soon to present itself.

A little boy near the tail end of the caravan was the first to look back and discover what he thought was shooting stars. His cry rang out above the din, "Falling stars! We are followed by falling stars!" Those immediately surrounding him stopped and looked back. It did, indeed, appear as if shooting of falling stars were following them, but the truth about these entities soon dawned on them. There appeared in the sky several glowing sparks which looked at bit like meteors—or shooting stars—but which quickly turned out to be something different altogether. As they came nearer it became apparent that these objects were not falling or shooting across the sky. They were, in fact, flying with terrifying speed, aiming for the line of refugees, then turning away at the very last moment, scattering people behind them and inciting fresh panic in the crowd.

"We are being attacked!" The shout from the rear of the caravan sounded all the way to the front and the soldiers promptly turned and faced towards the attackers. These turned out to be creatures resembling horses, but on fire or burning from within. They flew over the caravan and dive-bombed it, spreading small glowing tongues of flames that licked the skin of the people underneath them. This was excruciatingly painful for those that got hit by them, and they left red marks—sore to the touch—on the skin.

"Ghalorr!" Elderanna muttered under her breath, striding back to confront the new enemy. She did not stop to consider how she knew what they were; she knew, that was enough for now. In front of her, Rajan was clearing a path through the crowd of milling people, while at the same time ordering soldiers to protect the fleeing people from the flying menaces, with their bare hands, if necessary.

As they came to the end of the line, Elderanna faced the Ghalorr with a strange look on her face. Lifting her hands high and spreading her palms towards them, she sang. Tarlief, who had been right behind her, now joined her in chanting, and together they drove the Ghalorr back with a stinging wind that they conjured up from the south, a wind filled with frozen rain and cold. It was a spectacle that Rajan would never forget; the fire from the Ghalorr hitting the frozen raindrops and turning them into burning ice. Beautiful, but deadly, for the rain increased in strength and the raindrops became hailstones the size of balls. A few of the Ghalorrs were hit and crashed to the ground in showers of sparks, while the rest retreated quickly to the north, whence they came. Tired, Elderanna and Tarlief let their hands down and turned to Rajan, "Let us go on," Elderanna said, "they will be back, and we have a long way to go to safety." Tarlief and Rajan nodded, and while Tarlief went on ahead to bring the orders to the front of the convoy, Rajan put a blanket around Elderanna's shoulders and led her gently through the stunned crowds.

While the convoy started up again, a group of farmers from the surrounding homesteads, got together and started off into the bushes to the left of the main column. They walked fast, but stealthily, through the forest towards an enclosure in a clearing, not far off the trail the convoy was following. The animals from their farms were gathered there and they wanted to bring these with them if that was at all possible. Coming to the enclosure they opened the gate but noticed that the farm animals seemed nervous, stomping the ground and jumping skittishly around. They all stopped to listen, and what they heard terrified them, so much that they almost lost control over themselves, a low-pitched growling sound, with added snarls and wheezing sounds, could be heard under the animals nervous bleating and mooing.

Quickly, hurriedly, they led the panicking animals out from the enclosure and sped back towards the convoy and what they hoped was safety in numbers. Behind them they heard the ominous sound of something following them— something huge by the sound—and getting nearer with each stride. In a matter of seconds, panic struck among the men and they lost control over themselves. A run became a sprint, and then a mad dash, but the sounds from behind kept getting nearer and nearer. In a blind panic they almost ran straight through the group of soldiers that were coming to their assistance.

Two combat groups led by General Rajan surged past them and took up their stand on the path, not a moment too soon. A huge Greitsch, wild with hunger and mad with rage, thundered toward them. Many of the soldiers visibly blanched, but still they held their post. In front stood the only man who had faced one of these creatures before, Rajan. What he may have been thinking in that moment was impossible to say, but his actions spoke louder than words could. He wielded his sword with excellence and before long had the creature retreating before him, with the soldiers following close behind and spreading out in a fan that closed on the Greitsch. In a joint attack they pinned the monster down and put an end to it with their lightning bolts. Walking back to the convoy on shaky legs, but with radiant smiles on their faces, Rajan saw a new determination in his soldiers, a force that grew from within. *Good,* he thought, *we will need it, and more too if we are to survive this.*

Back in the caravan, he went looking for Mojastic without success. After some minutes of searching he asked Eythana, the nursemaid, in charge of the new-born prince. "I really can't say…" she started, but then she seemed to remember something, "Wait! I saw him go down to the river where we halted just some moments ago!" Quickly, Rajan made his way to the riverbank, and found Mojastic there, seemingly lost in thought. When he got nearer, however, he noticed that the king was shaking and when he strained his ears, he could hear him sobbing.

Insecure, Rajan halted his approach, and waited to see if his old friend would notice him. Mojastic did not give any outward signs of this, so he decided to go slowly forth and touched the king lightly on the arm. Mojastic held his breath for a second, then whispered, "I miss her! I miss her so much already; I feel like I am drowning in some hot liquid... Why??? Why now? Why her?" Abruptly, he turned around and flung his arms around Rajan, who, taken by surprise, had all he could do to keep them from falling. Stroking the king on his back and whispering soothing—but oh, so empty— words of consolation to him, he managed to calm Mojastic down after a while.

While his last sobs turned into sniffles, Mojastic smiled weakly to his companion of many hunting trips over the years, and said wryly, "Well, that would have been embarrassing if someone had seen us!"

Rajan's smile lit up his careworn face, "Seen what? I only see a man overcome by the fresh grief he just experienced. But I know in my heart that that man will rise all the stronger for it, not to forget his one true love, but to give her honour! And I do not mean to take away the time you need to grieve, I just think that the present situation is not the best time to lose yourself in it."

Mojastic nodded and looked at Rajan with a face transformed. Where there had been sorrow etched in every line, there was now a melancholy too deep for words, but also a newfound strength. "You speak truly, as always, and is it not true that a friend speaks the words that you need, but not necessarily the words you want to hear? You have put faith in my heart again, my friend, as well as the determination I need! Let us go and join the caravan, we must speed them up! I fear that evil things are behind us, and they are closing on us— fast!"

Having said this, they both hurried back to the convoy, Mojastic taking the lead and pushing everyone to increase their speed. Meanwhile Rajan went in search of Elderanna, and he found her in the company of Eythana and the little prince.

Prince Myrathion was evidently hungry from the sound he was making, but food had been prepared for him, a bottle of something which looked like milk had been heated to just the right temperature. Rajan arrived just as Elderanna succeeded in getting him to suck it, and from the look on his face, he was happy with the contents of the bottle. Smiling at Eythana and wishing her a safe journey onward, he led Elderanna out of earshot by the elbow, "We have to speed people up, the enemy is gaining on us from behind and I suspect they are also going to try to ambush us. I need for you to try out the elaidaring again and see what you can spot."

Elderanna looked back at the peaceful little scene with the prince and Eythana, then she looked at Rajan and nodded; "Yes, you are right. I will tell Eythana and the escort to speed up the pace, and then I will see what I can find out." Before long, Eythana and Myrathion were installed in a light wagon that sped along the track with the escort partly on horseback and partly running beside it, taking turns riding in the wagon with the prince.

Some minutes later, Elderanna was flying again. The speed of the wind and the feeling of freedom was so exhilarating to her that for a moment she just revelled in the feeling, but reality immediately intruded. From the north, she could see something resembling a dark wave break over the hilltop behind where she knew the castle stood, but the castle itself was engulfed in flames, with only the high turret visible.

The dark wave consisted of creatures of varying size and shape, but all of them with ferocious faces. Behind the convoy of fleeing people, she discerned a group of chasing enemies getting closer, but still about a mile away; she would have to alert Rajan to that situation. Looking ahead, at first, she could not see anything, but upon closer inspection she found some oddities in the landscape. Intrigued, she flew closer—slowly and carefully—and found an ambush, just where Rajan had said it might lie in waiting. She scoured the ground for a few more miles, but did not find anything, so she quickly sped back to give him the intelligence she had gathered.

Back in the convoy, she suddenly appeared beside Rajan while he was immersed in a conversation with Mojastic and the other generals. Needless to say, she scared the daylights out of them, appearing like that from thin air! Or, at least, that was what Mojastic said when he got his wind back. Rajan, who was after all expecting her, smiled secretly in his beard, but quickly got down to business. First, the three generals dispatched two divisions to deal with the pursuers, and then they started planning how to get the better of the ambush lying in wait ahead of them. In the end, they agreed to a manoeuvre where two divisions would circumvent the ambush, coming from behind on either side, while two units would come all the way around and behind the ambush, thus gripping them in a vice. "It might seem like overkill," General Trecon said, "but it is better to be safe than sorry!"

During the time they spent on these deliberations, Elderanna had taken to walking with some of the soldiers in front of the caravan, and while they walked, she asked one of them, who was the best singer. He pointed his finger at a female soldier right in front of them and winked at her.

"Taisha has the best voice I have ever heard, and it is big, as well as good!" Elderanna winked back at him and made her way to Taisha. Falling into stride beside her, she started humming an old battle-hymn that she learned when she first came to Arboria. Startled, Taisha looked at her, then smiled and started singing along. It was true; she had a remarkable voice. It rang through the convoy like a bell, and before many minutes had passed, people joined in and the sound of singing grew louder and clearer. "Keep it up," she said to Taisha, "it is good for morale, strengthens the mind and resolve, and gives courage to the faint of heart!" Taisha nodded affirmatively and brought her voice up another notch.

Coming back to the generals, she quickly concurred with their plan and set about finding her place in it as scout and magical 'enforcer,' as they called her. While she was thus occupied, she overheard Arcull talking to Mojastic, and something made her stop and listen. Now, the advisors had been coming and going since the caravan began, so there was nothing out of the ordinary in him seeing Mojastic. But...there was something in the tone of his voice...she turned back in search for Rajan, and, fortunately, found him within minutes. Together they went to see Mojastic, only to discover him still in dialogue with the advisor. Rajan approached them with measured steps, and with a polite greeting for Arcull. But the response was not what he was looking for.

Arcull appeared to be in something of a hurry, breathless and flustered, and he was angered by the intrusion—or so it appeared—of two more people in the discussion. He spat a greeting to Rajan, completely overlooked Elderanna, and continued his pleading with Mojastic, "This is madness! We have all seen what resistance is good for, you have seen it in your wife!" At this, Mojastic's face visibly darkened, but he did not say anything—yet. "The only chance we have, as a people, is to agree to his terms of surrender, and take our chances with him, bargaining for a better life when these animosities have ended!"

"So, you will take his terms and live the rest of your days as his slave!" Rajan thundered, unable to hold back his anger. "And how long, exactly, do you think you will last in that capacity?"

Furious, Arcull turned around and faced Rajan, "I will last longer than you, you filthy bastard! You and the other warmongers will be used for firing up the blaze inside the mountain, while the rest of the people will be outside, waiting for their reward!"

At this point, Elderanna could not hold back anymore, and she was just about to flay Arcull with her tongue, when Mojastic stopped her. With a stony face and blazing eyes, he stepped in front of Arcull, who looked as if he was shrinking in the king's shadow.

"What dare you call my best and truest general?" Mojastic said in measured tones, with an almost unnaturally quiet voice. A voice so still and yet so thundering, that everything around them went quiet. "And how do you know what will happen? Have you been talking to someone you had better let alone? Has the sorcerer gotten in your head, or did you invite him in?" his voice kept rising in volume, and by the ends of his utterance it was loud as thunder.

Arcull just stood there, frozen it seemed, in shock or in anger was not easy to tell. Then, suddenly, he screamed; the chilling scream of a banshee filled with hate and bitterness and threw himself at Mojastic with a knife in his hand. Rajan was lightning quick, however, and struck the knife aside with his blade. Arcull then turned tail and ran like a madman toward the line of trees the caravan had just cleared. "Let him run!" Rajan said, "We will soon meet him again, and then he will meet our justice!"

Seemingly echoing his words, the mountains started to rumble with a deep, dissonant sound, much like the low-pitched growl of a thousand tigers. Accompanying this was the sound of hissing or spitting, much as a snake, only magnified a million times. The column started to panic again, moving from side to side, some sections breaking into a run and other parts stumbling along as best they could. Rajan, bellowing at the top of his lungs, was able to calm things down and speed the caravan up, while at the same time posting two divisions at the back of the convoy to stem the tide if—or when—it overtook them.

Mojastic was on horseback again, ceaselessly riding back and forth along the caravan, encouraging people and giving them the extra strength to go on. Many took heart from his actions and in their turn encouraged others to do the same. Thus, they moved forward until there came a cry from the hill on their left. Out from under the trees came a band of soldiers, running—or fleeing—for their lives. It was, nevertheless, an organised retreat, at the back of the band came the officer, holding them all together and guiding them towards the caravan. Ordovan met them halfway down the hill with a fresh unit and guarded their flanks while they joined the rest of the refugees. Rajan and Trecon joined Ordovan and the officer—whose name was Elgar—with Mojastic. Elgar talked hurriedly but kept his voice down to not incite another panic,

"We were overrun, and barely escaped with our lives. There were other units too in that wood, but I do not know if they made it out. If they did, they will probably be waiting for us in the mountain pass or possibly on the other side of it."

Looking gravely at one another, Mojastic broke the silence and said, "We must keep a watch on the sides of the column as well as the front and back, but the most important thing we can do, is to increase our speed even further. All carts and wagons must be filled up with people who cannot walk fast—children, disabled, and elderly—and every beast that can be ridden must be employed. So, gentlemen, get to it!"

In a short while, the caravan became a fast-moving train, and in this way, they covered several miles before they had to take a break. Mojastic warned them, however, that it could only be a 'breather' that was all he would allow them before starting up again. Rajan was wiping his brow, he had been running the whole way and felt badly in need of catching his wind. Elderanna, who had also been on her feet the entire time, remarked that the exercise might be good for him, but she was smiling in a way that told him that she meant no harm. All the same, he got a little miffed at the insinuation, but then he smiled back at her; he saw the humour in the situation.

Suddenly, Rajan turned around—so quickly that he almost lost his balance. "What's that???" he exclaimed and pointed in the direction from whence they had come. What had caught his attention from the corner of his eye was a cloud that was forming over the trail some miles back, getting darker and more menacing by the minute.

"Everyone back on horseback and into the wagons!" Mojastic shouted, the turned to address his three generals, "We must increase security to our rear, what can you do?"

The three men looked at one another, then answered, in almost perfect unison, "We'll increase it with three divisions and three generals! Then, after you have reached the mountain pass, we will re-join the company and lead you safely from there." Hurrying back to the end of the column they gathered the divisions they needed, and when they reached the back of the column, they organised the soldiers according to the plan that had been hurriedly laid.

Rajan took one of the divisions and went back about a half-mile, then ordered the soldiers to walk in the shape of a rectangle while constantly changing places. This was to ensure himself that they would not get docile on their watch but keep constant vigilance. The line in back was scouring the sky, the lines on either side was half looking back, and to the side or to the front and side, and the line in front was looking forwards and to the sky; in this way they kept watch around the whole field of vision while at the same time moving forward at a reasonably fast pace. While they moved along the trail, they could hear sounds coming from behind and growing in intensity. Rajan looked desperately to the front where he could see a seemingly impenetrable mountain wall that looked as if it was running across the trail, blocking it from further progress. He knew this to be an illusion though, because just about a mile, perhaps shorter, down the path, it bent around a corner and then they would be able to see a deep cleft in that mountain wall. That was where he meant to make a stand and hold off the pursuers or turn them back, if that was possible.

By the time they reached the cleft, the pursuers were almost on their heels, so they only had time for throwing themselves in the pre-arranged positions and prepare for the onslaught. No sooner had they got their weapons ready, then the first wave broke around the corner. Surging towards the cleft was an unorganised mass of creatures: Daemoins, Greitsches and Drenkliches swarmed in the gully, pressing to be first through the cleft. They were met with a hail of arrows, spears, stones and lightning bolts. Screaming in pain and bewilderment the attack stopped and exploded into complete chaos; creatures trying to get back and escape from the stinging arrows collided with others trying to make their way through the cleft. 'Mayhem' could not even begin to describe the sight. There did not seem to be anyone in charge of the attackers, nor was there any plan in effect that the generals could recognise. They simply joined forces in a mass attack and that was that, not that it wasn't enough.

By the time the third wave hit, Rajan begun to realise that the problem was simply one of numbers; they could keep on coming like that all through the night and still have as many more to send in. He needed to come up with a solution that would hinder them long enough for the soldiers to get away and get back to the caravan, but what…? He suddenly became aware of a presence—not a threatening one—and turned around. Standing behind him was Elderanna. "How…?" was all he could say, then he realised that he probably would never understand the answer anyway.

She smiled and said, quite simply, "Do you need my assistance?"

He could have kissed her there and then but kept his head. "Yes! What could help immeasurably would be if you could somehow block their way with…something that would stop them or at least stall them for any amount of time! Can you do that?"

Elderanna smiled warmly—she guessed his thoughts—then answered, "Yes, I can do that, but I will need some assistance. Will you join me, please?" He nodded and quickly followed her up in the steep side of the cleft. When she found what she was looking for, she stopped and turned. "Can you lift that stone there for me?" she asked and pointed to a large boulder in front of them. He walked forward, squatted down and tried it, checking for handholds and weight.

"It is heavy," he said, "but I will try!" He then took hold of the boulder, got his feet in position under himself, and started to lift the immense boulder from the ground. Sweat dripped and ran from his body and veins stood out on his forehead, but he managed it. Lifting the boulder over his head, he stood there balancing the weight, and waiting for Elderanna to do whatever it was she was planning.

Behind him Elderanna had lifted her arms up—almost as if she was lifting the boulder too—and now she began to sing. It was a song in a language he had never, ever heard before. It rolled from her tongue like little pebbles dancing in a stream, and at the same time it glided as smooth a honey dripping from a beehive. He felt, more than he saw, the boulder that he held begin to burn, but he could not feel any heat. Then she spoke, "When I count to three, throw the boulder as far in front of you as you can manage, and I will do the rest."

He waited for her to count, and on three, he threw the boulder with all his might, up and out into the cleft. As it sailed through the air, it grew to immense proportions, and the fire burst like a volcano from it. It landed in the middle of the cleft, completely blocking the passage, and the flames from the boulder roared and rose sky-high. The enchantment that he felt, broke at that instant and he bellowed to his soldiers, "Retreat to the caravan, all of you! Quickly!"

While hurrying after the caravan, Elderanna told him of the events in the caravan since they left. It seemed that the influence of Arcull was deeper than they had thought at first, and there had been some difficulties with people arguing and wanting to surrender, "to save their lives," as they said, but the person that had talked them out of it was no other than Grimor. He had proven to be a great orator and had completely turned around the mood in the population. "I believe they would have turned back to fight if he had asked them," she said. Rajan listened in amazement, it was really a lot to take in, but it was hopeful news: they would really need someone who could direct the people if Mojastic did that which he feared he was planning.

When they re-joined the caravan, they found everyone in a somewhat uplifted mood; the news from the battle at the cleft had greatly stirred their hearts. It had also given them some breathing space, which was much in demand by now. Now, the caravan was nearing the summit of the trail: a mountain pass carved into the jagged, uneven edge of the mountain range. In front of the caravan, rode Mojastic, and when he rode through the pass, he felt a pang of remorse. He was leaving the land of his fathers, going as a refugee into an unknown world, where everything he knew would be altered, where he would be alone and facing unknown—even undreamed of—dangers. But he shrugged these thought off; he was not the only one in the caravan who had to bear heavy losses, and his heart ached for all of them as they made the transit into foreign lands.

When the caravan started the steep, downward journey, they entered lands that for most of them were completely alien. Trees, birds, animals, small growths, and bushes, everything was different and yet not. They found a lot of plants and animals that they recognised from home, some of which were refugees too, and many things in the new flora and fauna were familiar, or at least very closely related to their own, homegrown species. But a lot of the different varieties they encountered were entirely new to them.

"Look!" a woman in her thirties suddenly cried out. "There is one of the birds that was in the hall at the royal wedding!" And rightly, it was a beautiful bird with colourful feathers, ranging from deep green to bright red, flying gracefully above their heads, following the column as it wound its way down the mountainside. Mojastic ached inside at the sight of it; it was a memory of another world in different age. They lookouts were still in emergency mode and was keeping vigilance both ahead and in the rear, but so far there was no sign of followers or enemies lying in wait.

At length they entered the lowlands, a lush, green landscape of river plains, forests, and a burgeoning animal life. It was there that they met up with the Afamian army—or some of the remnants of it, anyway. At first, the sight of a large mass of soldiers sent the whole column into fight mode, but then General Trecon recognised one of the soldiers in front; a very big, young man whom he had had under his command earlier in the summer. This sent a wave of hope through the convoy; perhaps there could be more survivors? The mass of soldiers counted around six divisions and was being led by Aydra and Lyria, two officers who had managed to lead their divisions out of the battles without too many losses. They had also picked up other groups of soldiers on their way from the north western border, where the fighting had been hardest, among them quite a few units of Arborian soldiers who, fleeing from the onslaught, had been forced to traverse the mountains as they were unable to reach the trail.

When the officers met up with the king and generals, the first thing they did was update each other on the status in their respective countries—not an encouraging task, but it had to be done, as General Ordovan said. Mojastic had to tell them of the loss of Myra, which the Afamians took heavily. It was a dire blow to their hopes for the future, but when Mojastic presented for them Prince Myrathion, their countenances cleared and brightened. The little prince slept peacefully, completely unaware of his surroundings or his situation, while Aydra and Lyria bowed to him, and studied him closely, looking for likenesses to his parentage. Myrathion chose that precise moment to open his dark-grey eyes and look straight at them, which led Lyria to turn around and look closely at Mojastic, "Does Your Highness know what legacy his son has inherited?"

"Yes," answered the king, "I know and accept the inheritance, both its powers and its responsibilities." Hearing this, the officers bowed deeply to him. Rajan and his fellow generals looked on in puzzlement but decided that they would be informed when and if it was necessary.

After the formalities, the discussion centred on the current situation: where the refugees should be heading, where the army would be needed the most, and what should be done about the attack from the north. These deliberations lasted well into the night, and the caravan of refugees settled in for the night while the division in charge of the back of the column was on guard duty around the whole perimeter of the camp—such as it was. People could still see the lights from the king's tent when they settled in for the night, and they knew that the discussions going on were both, weighty and serious—discussions that would have consequences for them all. An hour before daybreak, the lights were finally put out and the officers, advisors, and other participants went to their resting places for a short while before the day started up again.

When the sun had risen and everyone was up and about, the king called for a general assembly. The crowd gathered around while the king stood on a large boulder in the middle so all could see him. Unfortunately, not everyone could hear his speech, but soldiers were placed at intervals through the mass of people, and when he made pauses, they would relate his words to the people around them, spreading the speech like ripples through water. He spoke slowly and clearly and took his time to get his message through, crystal clear and unequivocally, and though people cried at his words, their hearts were filled with determination to see this through—no matter what should happen in the future. He spoke for a long time, telling them where to go and what to do once they got there. He also told them who would be in charge and what should be done, and he told them who would try to do something about the dreadful situations they were in. He concluded, "So, in short, go south to Daitemia and do not tarry on the way. Let Grimor and his fellow advisors lead you; they are all trustworthy and deep in my counsels. Partake in the efforts made by the Daitemians to keep their country safe and prosperous and follow their requests as good guests. A small party of the army and some of the spell casters will follow me into the north to try and put an end to this reign of terror which we have been subjected to the last months."

Elderanna—who had been occupied elsewhere, gathering herbs and other plant for the expedition north—sighed. "What else could he say? That he was going on a journey of no return? Going to the slaughterhouse? Because that is likely to be the end of everything… Still, he has got to go, and we have to go with him, and that is that—end of discussion!"

Rajan wrapped her in his arms and kissed her on the nose without caring who or what may be looking, "Well, at least we will both be going with him, so I will get to hear a lot more of you!" Flustered and blushing, Elderanna tried half-heartedly to free herself, but did not look especially distraught at failing in this. She laughed at him and kissed him back— properly—and then employed her secret weapon, tickling him under the arms. Laughing, he let her go and turned around, only to discover Mojastic smiling secretively behind his back.

"I was wondering if you had time for what I hope will be a short discussion before we start on our crazed adventure," he smiled. Laughing and smiling, the couple followed him into his tent—the only one still standing; the rest had been taken down in preparation for the column's sortie. Before long, the caravan was ready to depart and Mojastic, Rajan, Elderanna, Ordovan, Trecon, and the remaining soldiers were out seeing them off. It was a strange feeling as they stood by the king's tent with what seemed like a flood drifting by them on either side, making it seem like they were standing on an island in the middle. People saluted Mojastic as they passed the tent, making it look like there was a ripple or small rapid in the river as it drifted past them. It took quite a while for the caravan to pass but pass it did, and by the time the last part of it was lost beyond the edge of the horizon, they had resumed their planning again.

Chapter 14
A Journey of Despair

Elderanna woke up in the early hours of the morning, and the night was still dark when she made her way out of the tent. Not that there was much light; even in the middle of the day a murky brown hue discoloured the sun and made the days colder than they should have been. There seemed to be a veil in front of the sun, or an almost transparent layer of...what? She shook her head in disgust: magic! That was what it was, and not benevolent either. She felt it in every fibre of her body and with every breath she took; it clung to her skin like some oily substance and made her food taste sour somehow. By looking at the others in her company, she knew that they felt a bit of the same sensations, albeit not so clearly.

Standing in front of the tent and looking out at the bleak dawn, she sensed her man coming out of the tent they now shared. Her man...how incredible, unbelievable, incredulous that sounded, and yet it had come to pass at last. Rajan came up quietly behind her and touched her shoulder, "Are you alright?" he asked, showing concern in every feature of his face. He had grounds for his concern; lately she had not been sleeping at all and he was afraid for the effect on her mental faculties. They needed her—he needed her—to be sharp and ready for action at any given time.

"Oh, I am fine," she answered, and smiled up at his worried face. "You must stop fretting over me. I do not need sleep like you do, in fact, it has been many years since I slept the way you think of sleep. But I can sleep in the daytime, or whenever I wish, by relaxing every part of my brain, while my vigilance is still being kept up. That way I get refreshed and rested, easily and efficiently." Again, she smiled, this time with a little mischievous twinkle in her eye. "But I thoroughly enjoy resting…by your side every night, my good man!"

Roaring with laughter and scaring up a flock of crows at the same time, he threw out an arm and clasped her tightly; "So do I!" he whispered hotly in her ear.

The rest of the camp, having been woken by Rajan's hearty laughter, now made their appearances, rubbing the sleep out of their eyes with or without an accompanying form of "Good morning!" Mojastic did not appear, however, so Rajan went to investigate his tent, but found it empty. Turning back towards Elderanna with a puzzled look on his face, he had just begun to ponder what might have happened, when the king appeared from the edge of the forest. He was carrying something on his back, something large and heavy from the look on his face. As he drew closer, they could all see what it was; a fine deer, two to three years old, and big enough to feed the whole company. "I woke early and decided to take a walk out to our guards," he said, "and on the way back I caught this one grazing in the middle of the clearing. I simply could not walk by without trying a shot!"

Turning to Elderanna, he laid the deer on the ground and asked, "Can you check it? It would be disastrous—and embarrassing for me—if it turned out to be a magic trick of some kind. I could wind up poisoning the company!"

Elderanna chuckled at that. "Yes, indeed it would be," she said, "so I will check it, but I sincerely hope it is the real thing!" While she took care of the deer, the rest of the camp began their daily routine. The council members were having a short meeting before breakfast, the guards met up and set up the day's roster, and those who were left—not many—made and laid out the breakfast. Not that it was in any way splendid, but it was healthy and filling and that was the main point.

As they sat down together to eat, the subject of conversation was the progress they had made over the last few days and what they expected to gain over the next week. Sure, they had covered some ground since they began the trek northward, but at the same time they all felt like they were 'dragging their feet' as it were. As General Ordovan remarked, "I have never swum in molasses, but I imagine it must feel like this, sticky, and clingy, and exhausting." There were nods of consent around the fire. Elderanna also agreed to this when she joined them, after concluding that the deer was in no way interfered with and could safely be prepared for that evening's meal, which they all looked forward to.

Mojastic smiled at her, "Then I count myself lucky," he said, "and look forward to a feast tonight!" Winking at him, she sat down and got handed a plate of greens and meat by Rajan, who had been preparing it for her arrival. Thanking him, she began to eat, as always slowly and deliberately.

When everyone had finished, Mojastic stood up and spoke, "According to our maps and the surveillance provided by our spell casters, we are now just one ridge from leaving the lands of Arboria. On the other side of this row of hills is the northern edge of Afamia, with tundra in wide plains. We have decided to walk in a half-circle around the eastern edge of Mount Dorth and approach it from the north side. This is the route which we think might be least guarded, as it is long and tedious and involves weary days on paths and roads that have mostly disappeared due to neglect and disuse. We might escape some watchful eyes if we take this route, but we know there are no guarantees, all roads may be watched, and any approach may end in carnage." His words fell heavy on their hearts, but they had signed up for this journey fully knowing it might end badly for all of them and they would not turn back now. And, besides, what could they turn back to? A life on the run? Or certain, premature death?

The group counted Mojastic, Elderanna, Rajan, Ordovan, Tarlief, Ingan, one unit—or twenty-five soldiers, of which Rhiann was one—and Theyn as their lieutenant. Thirty-two people in all, all of them devoted to their cause and their king, and all of them equally uncertain about what lay in store for them in the days ahead. As the only woman in a male party, one might expect Elderanna to seem small and in need of protection, but nothing could be farther from the truth. In the last weeks, Elderanna had seemed to grow in stature, in strength, in her aura, and in luminescence. She seemed to glow from within with a warm, rich, strong and, sometimes, burning flame that fed her being and resolve. In short, she seemed invincible. They all noted this change in her, for although the change itself had been subtle and slow, the results were immediate and powerful.

Her Elaidar was more powerful and immediate than ever, her spellcasting abilities outpaced anyone, excepting perhaps Mojastic, and she had begun showing other abilities too, like clairvoyance and 'shifting'—moving from place to place without travelling. She could move hundreds of metres that way, just popping up where she was least expected, and still she was rapidly getting stronger. She was remembering too, but this was something she only shared with Rajan, for the things she remembered were still so confusing to her that she did not want everyone to know. If someone had asked her what was going on, she would just have said, "I really do not know," but in her heart, she suspected, she knew. She was powering up and getting ready for the battle. And she was not the only one.

Mojastic felt—more than he knew—that he too was somehow changing, that his talents were being honed and tested. But he was nowhere near Elderanna's level of skills and kept his silence about it. Rajan was, as always, the trustworthy, steady soldier, companion and friend, but even he sensed that something was subtly changing, although he could not say exactly what. What the rest of the company felt, or sensed, had not been the topic of conversation, but they too had a raised level of awareness and alertness.

Following Mojastic's little talk they began to break camp and got ready for departure. In a triple line they filed onto the path and began their way toward the summit and over to the far side of the ridge. Within two hours' time, they had begun their descent into the plains on the northern edge of Afamia and were on foreign ground, as none of them had ever been here before.

Hour upon hour went by, and the landscape floated by them—unchanging. It seemed like they were stuck on a river that floated in a huge circle and kept coming back to the same place. No landmarks could be identified, and no ripples could be seen, only flat, tedious tundra wherever they turned. Of course, they could still see the line of mountains behind them, but even that had shrunk into a slightly darker line just above the horizon, and besides, they did not intend to go back. Mojastic, who had been going in front of the company the whole morning, was beginning to get a queasy feeling in his stomach; something was off. The problem was, there was not a single problem in sight. Still the feeling grew, and when Elderanna suddenly shifted from wherever she had been to his side, he almost screamed from the shock. "Something is out there," she said, "something very bad."

Mojastic looked at her and asked, "Can you see what it is?"

"No," she replied, "but I can try to lure it out into the open. But if I am to do that, archers and lance men will need to be ready. You see; I have a feeling I know what this is." Mojastic did not need any more prompting, he immediately called for the soldiers to be ready for action.

Quickly, Elderanna then explained what she was about to do, and while the eyebrows of those close enough to hear her plan, slowly regained their allotted space in their faces, she set the plan into motion. She began with casting a spell that she had never tried out before—as far as she could remember—but which, nevertheless, felt very familiar. As her song rose to the sky, the soldiers began to see duplicates of themselves materialising next to them and growing more and more 'solid' as the spell was woven tighter. This shadow-company then proceeded to march forward on the trail, walking ahead of the real company, but looking so real that many of the soldiers were pinching themselves to ensure that they were not dreaming. Elderanna signalled for them to keep their distance and let the shadows get a little ahead. This proved to be a good thing, for suddenly the attack was unleashed and havoc broke loose. It came seemingly from nowhere. A gigantic worm-like creature burst out from the sandy ground where it had been hidden, froth and spittle raining from its cavernous mouth, attacking with lightning speed and devouring much of the shadow company before either of the men had their bows or lances ready. Fortunately, the creature was so pre-occupied with the decoys that the real soldiers were given time enough to get into attack formation and take on the challenge. Arrows hailed over the creature, which hissed and spat ferociously at them, but could not reach any of them, and when the lance men took over it was subdued and eventually vanquished.

Standing over the carcass and looking closely at what seemed like a living nightmare, Rajan and Mojastic exchanged meaningful glances before asking Elderanna, "What in the world was this creature? Monster? Animal? Some being we have never met or heard of, surely?"

"No," she answered sadly. "This is what happens when someone tries to alter beings in order to bring about better warriors, or servants, or weapons…" She trailed off; her voice sad. Over her head they sent puzzled looks at each other and Rajan was about to ask her what she meant, when she continued, "Look closely. What does it remind you of?" They looked again, but whatever she was referring to, eluded their attention completely. In the end, she showed them, "Look here, do these rings around its body remind you of something? And what about these rudimentary feet?"

When she drew their attention to the body parts, Rajan's eyes lit up in understanding, "It is a centipede! But what made it grow to this enormous size? And what forces altered it into a nightmare?"

"I believe it is one of the many inhabitants of Mount Dorth or the lands beyond it. As for what has changed it, I do not know, not yet at least." Elderanna sounded sorrowful and thoughtful. Leaving the men standing around the monstrous centipede, she went to her bundle and picked it up. "Gentlemen," she said, "time is running and waits for no one! Let us get going, so we can find a campsite before it gets dark. I want that meal tonight, more than ever, and I know we all deserve it after this ordeal!"

Two weary weeks later, they were no nearer to their goal than they had been, or so it seemed. The landscape stretched out before them in an endless, wide expanse, gently undulating toward the horizon. Not a landmark could be seen, nothing to rest your eyes upon, just more of the same. The soldiers' eyes had long since glazed over in boredom, and even the officers' gaze had some of the same blank quality. Of all the company, only Elderanna still had as sharp an eye as ever, but even she was beginning to feel the weight of hundreds of hours of constant vigilance. The path went straight ahead to the horizon, and perhaps this was the cause of their weariness.

Nothing is more tiresome than a straight line! Elderanna thought. She felt sleepy too, the sort of heavy sleepiness that saps your limbs of all vigour. Probably another reaction to boredom. She yawned, and noticed one of the soldiers stumbling, just barely regaining his balance. *Now, what was that?* She wondered, and then shocked them all awake by screaming out loud, "WAKE UP!" It was just in time, or almost just in time. In the horizon, a cloud appeared, travelling extremely swift and spreading out as it came. As it blasted nearer, they could see the individual shapes of a herd of Ghalorr. It all happened in a matter of seconds; one moment they spotted the cloud, the next moment they were trying to shield themselves from the rain of fire from the sky.

The moment stretched into infinity, or at least it felt that way. Around her the soldiers were screaming in pain and terror, with some of them doing their best to shoot down as many as possible of the flying horrors. Elderanna found herself slow in gathering her wits about her but managed to summon up the spell she used the first time the Ghalorr attacked. By her side stood Mojastic, and now his capacity really was put to the test. Elderanna was shocked by the power he revealed in himself, but as it was an untrained spellcaster and enchanter that stood beside her, his contribution to her effort was mostly raw strength. In the end, however, that was what drove them away.

When the last Ghalorr was out of sight and they could breathe again, came the time for surveying the damage caused by the ravaging fire, soldiers' bodies lying everywhere, some wounded, some crying, some burnt to cinders. And not only soldiers, Ingan and Tarlief were both hurt and could no longer go on, but Ordovan had sustained the worst damages. Lying on the ground, heaving for breath, it was clear that these were wounds from which he would not recover. He had been in the front line and had fought bravely, instilling courage in the men beside him but, in the end, he had been overpowered and run into the ground. Mojastic was kneeling beside him, while Rajan did his best to comfort him where he lay. Elderanna sat down by his head and whispered something to him—just a few words—that made the dying man smile up at her through his pain, and then it was over. Silence fell over the remaining company, only broken by the sobs from the wounded men.

After long moments had passed, Elderanna stood and called for all to pay attention. Weary faces, grim with tears and pain, met her gaze wherever she looked. "We have to go on," she said simply. "But not all of us, maybe just a few, the rest must go back and join the others in time." She had quietly taken control over the situation, but no one argued with her, it felt natural that the strongest person in the group should lead in times of dire need. First, she called upon the able-bodied soldiers—six in all—to come forward and prepare a grave for the fourteen men who had been killed in the skirmish, then she called upon the wounded councilmembers to lead the soldiers back to the south. She told them to take the straightest route possible and wait for no man on the way. After finishing giving orders, she turned to Mojastic and Rajan who were standing behind her. "Well, my friends, are you ready for the longest lap of the journey?" Both men nodded in consent, and as if they had been released, the whole company—or what remained of it—went about the chores she had given them, and before long, the party were ready to part ways.

Looking at the band accompanying Ingan and Tarlief, she smiled a little sadly, then, signalling that they should start, turned away from them and faced north together with her two companions. "Well," she said, "Is there something special you are waiting for, or are you ready to continue?"

"As ready as I will ever be!" answered Rajan, while Mojastic merely smiled a little and nodded. Setting one foot ahead of the other, they started on their journey as the first stars opened in the sky above them.

They kept walking at a brisk, steady pace until the moon had set, and then set up camp as quickly as they could. Mojastic volunteered for the first watch, and when the other two nestled up under the cover, they could see him—a black shadow against the dark sky—pacing back and forth behind the glow of the dying fire. Then their eyes closed, and their minds went mercifully quiet.

When they awoke the next morning, both felt that something was awry. "Why has not Mojastic woken either of us for the next watch?" Rajan asked with a frown. "This is not like him at all!" He rose to his feet and started looking around for the king. Elderanna, who had jumped up as soon as she opened her eyes, stood quietly listening, eyes closed, and feeling her way for Mojastic's aura.

"He is nowhere to be found," she said at last, "at least not as far as my mind can reach."

Rajan stopped and stared at her, "What does that mean?" he demanded.

"It means that he cannot be found," she replied patiently. "Either it can be a mishap: his abilities—wholly new to him— have been overstimulated and have sent him into a trance and carried him away somewhere—most likely ahead of us. Or it can be his own, conscious doing, he has gone off on his own and does not want us to follow—to keep us from the worst of the danger ahead. Or it is someone else's doing, and they want to separate us—to deal with us separately and in their own time, so to speak. At present I cannot say, your guess is as good as mine."

If this had been only a month ago, Rajan would have been flabbergasted, but now he had gotten used to Elderanna and her straightforward ways, and so all he said was, "So? What do we do?"

"The only thing we can, of course," she replied, "We go and search for him!" And with that settled, they quickly broke camp and were on their way—ever northward.

Chapter 15
The Crow's Song

When Mojastic awoke he was all alone and, in the beginning, utterly confused. Where was he? Where were the others? What had happened? The landscape that met his eyes was almost totally brown with just a hint of different shades in it. A fine dust flew up in even the slightest breeze, making his eyes sting and water. Also, it was totally devoid of life, as far as he could see. He rose to his feet, staggering a little because of stiff and sore muscles—never sleep directly on the ground, he told himself—and tried to recall what had happened the evening before. While his mind raced through the events of the previous day, his eyes scanned the landscape around him for signs of life, but to no avail. What had he done? He vaguely remembered taking the first watch of the night and being unable to sit down, he had been pacing the perimeter of their camp—small as it was—and thinking about the journey ahead of them and the perils that lay in store. And some time after Rajan and Elderanna had drifted off to sleep, he had…what? Fallen asleep while walking??? He shook his head in confusion; how could that be possible? He recalled having vivid dreams of walking or…speeding across the landscape without touching it. How had he done that? And were they dreams or memories? He had been…thinking, and then he had…elaidared? His eyes widened. No! That could not be…or could it?

Shaking his head vigorously to get rid of the fog that he felt was in it, he opened his eyes again and looked at the landscape in earnest. Drab and dreary it was, but the ground was now rising in little ripples, here and there breaking up in canyons—albeit very small so far—all leading in the same general direction, northwest. That would mean that he was several miles further north than he had been when they struck camp! He sighed, thinking of the two he had left behind, but concluded that they were as able to take care of themselves alone as together with him, perhaps better. As he had landed in this situation without any of his gear, he would have to find water as well as food soon, or he would be in more trouble than he already was. Seeking for water was his number one priority and with that thought in his mind, he started walking north again. Following him, so high in the air that it only seemed a speck of dust, was the lonely figure of a crow. If he strained his ears, he could hear it cawing away, almost like a tiresome camp song, with way too many verses in it. The crow and its monotonous song kept him company for most of that day.

Many miles further south, Rajan and Elderanna were walking in the same direction but as they had all their gear—and Mojastic's as well—their store of food and water was plentiful for now, but that did not mean that their journey was without its problems. Trudging along, Rajan felt his feet complaining like they never had before. Yes, he was used to campaigns and marches and heavy duties, but not like this; his feet were covered in blisters and quite a few of them had broken open and were oozing puss into his shoes. Elderanna was walking next to him without saying a word, deep in thought. But when he suddenly stopped, unable to go any further without a short break and some bindings for his feet, she was on the case without even asking him what his problem was. Hurriedly unpacking her salves and ointments, she concocted a treatment that would have his feet, "singing with joy," as she put it, within the space of half an hour! Leaning back against a sleeping roll. Rajan closed his eyes and just enjoyed being cared about for a little while, indulging in the feeling of relaxed and cool feet.

Mumbling and grumbling, he got to his feet again after the break she allowed them but found to his satisfaction that she had not exaggerated the efficiency of her treatments. As he shouldered his backpack he remarked, "It is a pity we cannot fly! That way we could have covered huge tracts of land with less effort, and we would be safer as well!"

Elderanna stopped dead in her tracks, "What was it you said?" she enquired.

"I was just joking…" Rajan began but was cut short by her exclaiming, "You are a genius, my good man, and worthy of a kiss!" She was as good as her word, and while Rajan struggled to get his breath back, she was busy preparing their sacks and rolls, securing them tightly to prevent their loss.

Then she turned to him, "That is, of course, what Mojastic has done, whether in his sleep or awake, I do not know, and now we are going to attempt the same!"

Rajan blanched at the suggestion, and swallowing hard he asked in a somewhat quivering voice, "You mean, fly? Like your elaidaring? Both of us?"

With a radiant smile she answered, "That is exactly what I mean! Now, take my hands." He stepped closer, reluctantly holding his hands forward.

Smiling gently now, she took his hands in hers, gripped them tightly, and gave her instructions, "First, close your eyes and picture a candle in the wind. When the candle is blown out, follow the flame up in the wind and feel the warmth around you. Do not open your eyes until the shivering has ceased. You must not open them before you are mentally ready, ok? That would be dangerous for both of us!"

He nodded, a little bit insecurely, and she tiptoed up and kissed him full on the mouth, "I have full confidence in you, my good man! Now, let us fly!"

Mojastic could not remember ever having been this thirsty before. His mouth and throat were so parched, they felt like the surface of a sand-cliff, and it hurt to swallow or even draw air. He was hungry as well, but the main problem was the thirst. In the distance, he imagined he could see a brook running in the bottom of a shallow canyon, but when he got closer it proved to be just another dry bed where once water had been running. Sitting down heavily, he felt weak and desperate. It was not the heat that was doing this to him; the temperature was pleasant enough, though chilly at night, but the arid dryness of the air itself was enough to completely dehydrate him and leave him feeling parched and dried out. Looking around himself, he suddenly noticed a fleck of green colour in the brown grass next to the dry riverbed. He went over to investigate and found something rare in this environment: a tuft of grass, green as the freshest shots in spring, and with a reservoir of water in its roots! Drinking deeply from the plant, he did not care if the water tasted metallic and sour, it was life! Putting the plant back into its little hole in the ground and patting the soil back around the roots, he felt more himself again, and with that came the thought that made him slap himself in the forehead, *Why have I not been elaidaring?* In that moment, he felt more of an ass than any animal in his stables...

Moments later, he was floating along over the landscape, relishing the feeling of wind on his face while searching the terrain for huntable game or roots and berries. The crow, which had been keeping him company, fled in terror when he suddenly took to the air, and was not seen, nor mercifully heard, again on his journey.

When Rajan and Elderanna arrived at the same dry bed, they could sense that Mojastic had been there, but many hours earlier. Although they were encouraged by the thought of Mojastic being alive and somewhere up ahead, Elderanna had need of rest by the time they landed, and so they made camp and settled down for the night, snuggling together for comfort and solace.

Meanwhile, the returning group with the councilmembers and soldiers were half-heartedly making their way south, hoping to escape the eyes of the many creatures and enemies that were out and about. By fortunes' good will, they managed to get out of the open terrain without incident, and three days later found themselves in open woodlands, typical for the centre of Afamia. Slow-flowing rivers, deep lakes, a wholesome feeling in the air, and soft forest floors healed many of their wounds and ailments by the time they came to more inhabited lands. Joining up with a unit from the Afamian army, they made their way to the rest of the refugees with only a couple of skirmishes along the way.

Far to the north, Elderanna and Rajan were always a little behind Mojastic as the weeks went by, but they were confident he was there from the little signs and traces they could find. The land was steadily growing more inhospitable, an ice-cold desert seemingly devoid of life and water. The topography of the land was also changing, as they drew further north. The canyons were deeper and ran longer into the hills, and in addition, the shadow of Mount Dorth now loomed in the west, a monstrous black cloud covering the horizon. To make matters worse for the travellers, the provisions were running low and replenishments were scarce and far between. In all, not a cheerful situation for anyone, and that was by day. By night, the air was filled with eerie sounds of unseen creatures, many of which sounded as if they would not want to see them, and when they did catch a glimpse, it was of a shadow, shades darker than the night that surrounded them, and then they did not want to be seen. As Rajan put it, "There are things in this world that are out of this world, and there are things that should never have been in it. I think these shadows belong to both categories."

Mojastic, who was after all alone, was by far the one who had suffered most from the lack of water and provisions. Water he had found, although not nearly enough, but the lack of provisions was showing; if you saw him without his shirt on, you could count his ribs. Elderanna and Rajan went hungry every day, but they were not as badly off as Mojastic. The one thing that bothered all three of them though, was the cold. It was eating its way into their bodies and sapped them of the strength they so badly needed to get through the days, like it had a malevolent mind of its own. Fact was, it felt like the land itself was averse to their passing and did what it could to make their journey as crooked and uncomfortable as possible.

As a long day of flying through hostile skies over hostile lands came to an end, and the weary trio settled down to yet another night of cold slumber on the hard ground, they sensed a rumbling in the ground. They all sat up and looked to the west, and as another tremor came through the ground, they could all see the orange sheen over the shadow that stood there, so immense it even blocked out the stars.

As the trio slept, the skies above them opened up an awe-inspiring spectacle. Although the land seemed devoid of life forms and had precious few plants, the skies were a different matter. They had seen birds during their journey, not many, but they were present, small birds that reminded them of sparrows, and large birds that were predators of some kind. Being diurnal creatures, they had mostly gone to rest now, but the skies... They were lit up by a display of northern lights that spread out over the entirety of the expanse, and shone in brilliant colours: green, blue, red, yellow, orange, pink, purple, the whole rainbow was presented up there. In addition, the mountain to their right lit up the night with orange and dark red flares and rays. It was a magnificent sight and it went on for hours, until the light was once again returning in the east.

Chapter 16
The Big Empty

"The autumn equinox, that is it!" Rajan almost fell out of his blankets at the sound of Elderanna suddenly exclaiming in the early hours of the morning.

"Wh…what?" he stuttered, completely nonplussed by her words. "It is the autumn equinox today! One out of two days in the year when the night and day is of equal length, and a very important day in magic lore!"

"Oh…" was his answer, and by the look on his face he was still in the dark as to what she meant.

"On this day," she began, "important ceremonies are carried out, and peace-talks or deliberations are supposed to be most fruitful. In addition, the power of a wizard or witch— or sage if you like that better—can be doubled if certain rites are performed at the rising and setting of the sun."

This time realisation dawned on his face, "So, we can expect our adversary to be busy with his rituals?" he enquired.

"Yes," Elderanna answered, "but we can also perform some of our own. No reason to give him an advantage, or what?"

"No, definitely not!" he answered with some force.

"That is more like it," she laughed.

"I was beginning to worry you had lost yourself up there in the air!" This called for a wry smile on Rajan's part, he had had some initial problems with the flying sessions. Coming to terms with flying around in the air like a bird, when he did not have any wings...madness! But he had gotten used to it, and by now he was even enjoying it a little.

Elderanna quickly got down to business, and soon Rajan found himself running around gathering what herbs and grasses he could find and preparing for the ritual that Elderanna was going to perform. Of all the different roles he had pictured himself in, being assistant to a witch was never in the picture. It was enough to make him laugh out loud as he went about his business. Elderanna looked at him, puzzled, but did not ask what was going on; she was too busy herself, getting ready. She was thinking to herself that it was a good thing she had gathered many of the ingredients before they left Arboria and Afamia behind—otherwise she would not have been able to conduct the rites. As it was, it proved to be just barely enough together with what Rajan manged to scrape up from the dry, hard ground.

Many miles north from there, Mojastic woke up, frozen to the bone and shivering. The ground beneath him was frozen solid and his clothes offered little protection. Getting to his feet, he first surveyed the horizon as he had become accustomed to. Nothing could be seen, at least nothing living, but there was plenty to take in nevertheless, sandstorms— some quite recent—had left dunes where the ground was rising, making it even more difficult to traverse. A snowstorm was brewing in the northwest, filling up the skies above with dark grey clouds, tall and threatening. The vegetation that could be found—short, coarse grass and stunted trees—was mostly dead or dying; the arid climate saw to that, and there was not a living thing to be spotted, near or far. He sighed, took a sip from his water flask and chewed on the only food he had found these last days, dry, old roots that gave him the feeling of chewing on old tree-twigs. Well, it could not be helped, he had to eat something. By the time he was ready to go on, snow was falling. He stretched out his tongue as if he was a little boy again and caught a snowflake on the tip of it, he then tasted the snowflake and came to the inevitable conclusion; even the snow was dry in these lands. He sighed yet again: what had he expected? The land, its inhabitants, and the adversary waiting for him along the line, none of them was going to make this easy for him. Wearily, he took to the winds again.

Unbeknownst to them, they had entered the land of Nadara, more commonly known as Maigarr, at least the surface area. Underneath their feet could be found the other half, known to its inhabitants as Dorthnonder, but as this was a totally secretive and unexplored area, nothing was known about it. Above ground it was a desolate place as they had already found out, the only thing that lived there was birds. Maigarr was also inhabited by ghouls, but as these were generally shy and kept to themselves, none of the travellers had made their acquaintance yet.

What was present in the land of Maigarr, was Mount Dorth. Over the last week, the mountain had grown to unfathomable size and covered the whole horizon to the west, stretching not only over their whole field of vision, but also up into the clouds. It had a chilling effect on their minds, almost paralyzing, and it was ever present in their thoughts and dreams, or nightmares. The canyons—all pointing toward the mountain—had grown deeper and steeper; they now resembled gorges, and if they had walked like they had planned, they would long since have been stopped and had to turn back.

Mojastic—who had been alone on most of this journey—had had time to study the ground intently while he flew, and he had noticed that over the last days there had been ripples that seemed to be moving, but when he turned his eyes on them, they were completely still. It made him question his own eyes, until he thought more closely about it. It was just such a thing that the enemy could be expected to do, to throw him off his course, and make him loose his mind. Or perhaps he had already lost it? He chuckled over that thought for a while, before redirecting his attention to searching the landscape. While he floated over canyons and dunes, his mind returned to the creatures that had attacked them in Arboria. Where had they come from? Staring down at the brown, desolate lands beneath him, he knew the answer was right in front of him, he just had not found any evidence to back it up yet.

Elderanna and Rajan were also thinking along the same lines, flying over the web of canyons beneath them, but as they were talking together, they were quicker at coming to the same conclusions. "But there is something I do not understand," Rajan said. "Why have we not seen any of the creatures we assume must be here? Why, we have not even seen traces of them, and we have been keeping watch!!!"

"I do not know for sure," said Elderanna, "but something has been bothering me since we met up with that centipede."

"Centipedes, and flying snakes, and giant lizards; what do they have in common?" Rajan grumbled.

"They seem like fairy-tale monsters to me, but they have to come from somewhere, and this is the best candidate we have found so far. Except here is nothing!"

"Excuse me," said Elderanna, wonder in her eyes, "could you repeat the list?"

"What? Centipedes, and flying snakes, and giant lizards?" said Mojastic baffled.

"Yes! Oh, wonderful man, there you go again, finding the right question when we are in the dark! Of course, now I understand!"

"But I do not," said Mojastic, "I feel as darkened as ever despite your enthusiasm on my behalf!"

She laughed, a free, ringing and contagious sound, "Oh, my dearest, think, where do the creatures you mentioned live when we encounter them in our world?"

He looked at her with dawning realisation in his eyes, "Underground and in caves!" he answered. "Under rocks and in cracks in the mountain. I believe we have found them or, at least, we will. But how can we get down there without being seen?"

"After we have performed the rites at sundown tonight, we will discuss that," said Elderanna confidently.

When the sun set, Mojastic was nearing the ends of his day's journey, feeling totally exhausted. It was not the journey itself that was taking its toll, it was the endless plains with crags and canyons repeating itself over and over. If ever a landscape could be said to be tedious, this was it. The thing he was reminded of, was a nightmare where he was running down a corridor—it could be anywhere: the attic, the basement, the dungeons, or the kitchens—and the corridor seemed to stretch out forever while you had something evil behind you and you could not get away.

"Only this is not a dream, and the evil is in front of me, not behind." Slowly, he headed for the ground where he would set up camp, as meagre as it was, and try to get another night of broken sleep. He did notice on his way down that the crack and crags had become more numerous the last hour, and he was also aware that where he had been going due north, he was now bending more toward the northwest, following the curvature of the mountain looming to his left.

As he touched ground and became visible once more, he became aware of tracks in the sand. These were glowing faintly, and when he investigated them closer, he found out that they were in fact smouldering, as if a fiery being had walked in the sand or the thing leaving the tracks had been set on fire. But for the tracks to still be smouldering, that would have to have happened recently, and he had not seen anything moving down here while he had had it in his sights. Looking warily around the immediate surroundings he could not find any traces or more tracks from whoever it was that had put them there in the first place, so he had to settle for the night without any answers. It took him a long time to fall into a slumber, though, and that was what he got the rest of the night, slumbering with one eye open and alerted by any sounds that could be heard.

After the rites were finished, Rajan and Elderanna sat down on either side of the little fire they had going. Rajan was intent on following Elderanna's instructions, to minimise the risks involved in what they were now attempting. "What we are going to do, is to travel into the underground much the same way as we do when we are elaidaring, but this time we will have to leave our bodies behind."

"Like sinestraling, you mean? So effectively, we are going to be unprotected while we explore?" Rajan asked.

"No," said Elderanna, "we will be invisible to anyone who passes our campsite, but we will not have our bodies with us; they will be left here." Rajan looked a little uncomfortable at that, but he had no options, other than remaining behind, and that was out of the question.

Sometime later, they were ready to start and Elderanna took the lead, guiding them safely through the phases of the process. Rajan felt a peculiar sensation, like his whole body was crawling with ants, and then he felt his astral-being releasing itself from his physical body, floating free while he was left motionless on the ground. Involuntarily, he reached for himself, but a gentle nudge from Elderanna stopped him, "Do not worry," he heard her voice in his head, "we will still be here when we return." His mind spinning and trying to come to grips with this, he followed her into the underworld.

While Rajan and Elderanna were on their little expedition, Mojastic was sleeping fitfully—if it could be called sleep—tossing and turning every time a sound or sensation disturbed him. He was also being watched. Unbeknownst to him, one pair of eyes, glowing embers in the night, were watching his every move, heave and restless grunt. They stared at him, unceasingly, for at least half the night, before the embers were put out, just as dawn's first approach was signalled by the harsh cry of a large bird, high up in the air. When Mojastic woke up, as tired as when he went to sleep, no trace of the owner of the eyes could be seen anywhere.

Chapter 17
A Wanderer's Tale
and Strange Occurrences

When he awoke, he was completely disoriented and bewildered by the change in the scenery; all he could see was white-grey, woolly and diffuse. A thick, heavy fog was clinging to everything, soaking his clothes and shoes, and making his hair stick to his scalp and get in his eyes. In short, he felt miserable. Also, flying would be out of the question in this weather; he knew neither how high up this fog went, nor would he be able to see the ground underneath him in order to find a safe place to touch down again. In short, it was back to his feet again.

Starting off at a steady, but not too fast, pace, he covered a few miles before his first obstacle. A canyon appeared out of nowhere and he had to climb down a treacherous wall on one side and back up on the other. It was tedious work, and it took time and effort, and by noon he was utterly exhausted. Sitting himself down with his back against a boulder on the edge of yet another ravine, he suddenly noticed something peculiar on the other side. It did not appear to be anything other than a boulder at first, but when he looked at it more closely, he saw that it resembled the figure of a man, sitting down all huddled together. Amazed and alarmed at the same time, he stood up and surveyed it more thoroughly, he could clearly see its legs and the arms wound about the knees, but its face was covered by a hood. Suddenly, full of adrenaline and energy, he decided to hail it and see what happened.

He had just opened his mouth to call, when the stranger spoke, "Hail wanderer, where are you coming from and where are you going?"

Taken aback, he answered, "My name is my own, and I am on my way north. Who is asking?"

"The lord of nowhere," was the answer.

"Will you not come over here? I have food fit for a weary wanderer, and water to refresh you."

The offer came so abruptly that Mojastic was taken by surprise. He was hungry, yes, and thirsty, and he almost ran over without thinking, but then he steadied himself, "The ravine-wall is very steep here, and it is going to take me some time to get over there. Perhaps you know a speedier way to get here? You seem familiar with these lands."

The stranger laughed at that, "Well, what do you know! A hungry man with his mind still intact. But so be it, I will come over and bring my food and water with me!" At that, he stood up and sort of slid down the wall on his side, and then, in just three bounds, he was standing on the edge just a couple of metres from Mojastic.

For a while they just stood there, measuring each other, trying to get a feel of each other's strengths and weaknesses, but then they visibly relaxed and met halfway, stretching out their hands in a greeting. They ventured to sit down, and Mojastic lit a fire, noticing the mesmerised look from under the hood, while the lord of nowhere laid out the food and water for their meal. It was excellent fare, or so it seemed for the one who had been hungry for the better part of a month, and Mojastic had to keep telling himself to slow down and eat like a civilised man. He wondered a bit about the lord that did not eat much, but then again, he might have eaten before their paths crossed. Finally, he sat back and sighed with pleasure, his body for once feeling properly fed and watered, and directed his attention to the lord's face. Being in the shadow of the hood it was hard to read his expression, but his body language spoke of satisfaction with the way his gift had been received.

"So, lord, what brings you to these parts?" Mojastic opened the conversation and half expected a convoluted answer but was surprised when the lord answered candidly, "I have been sensing your presence for a while but have not had the skills to track your movements until this day. When I saw you, I followed your steps and decided to make contact here, where we are secluded and private in our dealings. Many eyes are scouring these lands, and not all would like us to meet and exchange words. Also, I was curious as to what could make a man come to these lands and what he could be searching for?"

Mojastic smiled, "Well," he said, "I believe I have sensed your presence also, although to be frank, I have not been able to pinpoint your whereabouts until you chose to reveal yourself to me."

"You are much too modest," replied the lord, "but be that as it may, you still have not spoken about your business in these parts."

"That would be because I do not believe that they concern you. My business in with another person, and it is not a going to be a pleasant rendezvous! His actions took the light of my life from me, and he will pay a heavy price for that, in addition to damages he owes my people!"

"I see," said the lord. "So, you know where to find him then?"

"I have a good idea, but I may have to search a little. From what I have seen, he is not a man who is easily caught at home." The lord smiled a little at that but did not say anything. He rose to his feet at this point and thanked Mojastic for his company.

"Maybe we will meet again," he said, "when we can sit and talk all night at leisure."

"That would be a pleasure," answered Mojastic, "and I would like to extend my gratitude to you for the gifts of food and water. The hunting has been less than plentiful these last weeks!"

"Yes, I can see that. It takes some time to learn how to find and hunt food here, but it is there if you know where to look."

Mojastic too rose to his feet and extended his hand in a farewell gesture, which the other was quick to take. Wishing each other good journey and good fortunes, they parted company, and the lord quickly disappeared in the fog, vanishing without a trace. The only proof that he had been there at all, was the water skins and bag of provisions he had left behind for Mojastic to keep.

Miles behind him, the bodies of Elderanna and Rajan were sitting motionlessly beside the campfire, while the owners of the bodies were scouting out the underworld. It was a splendid sight with cave after cave of various sizes and shapes flying past them as they sped along. They could see the glitter in the walls of gold, silver and precious stones, and the ever-changing colour scheme in the rock walls and ceiling of the caves, formed by the many types of stone that had been incorporated in their making. And suddenly, they found life. In a cavernous hall, where they could not see the other side, they ran into a congregation of some kind. It looked as if they were in the middle of a ritual of some sort although neither of the scouts could say what it was. The group of creatures was a varied lot, many of which they had already met. Greitsches, Drenkliches, and Daemoins were plentiful, as well as other beings that they had never encountered before. Floating above the congregation, they felt nearly invincible on account of being invisible, and therefore they took their time studying the many creatures intently. What became evident, however, was that the creatures that they could see, could also see them! Suddenly, a roar rose from the crowd and the chase was on. Never had Elderanna, nor Rajan, flown so fast! It was a regular slalom between the many obstacles on their way back to the surface, guards and angry beings were everywhere, and attacks came from every direction. Still, the two spies made it out in the open just in time. They reconnected with their bodies quicker than Elderanna found advisable but given that the pursuit was hard on their heels, they really did not have much choice. Getting to their feet, running around gathering their belongings and taking to the air, was a matter of minutes, but it was close to being too long, anyway. Just as they left the ground and became invisible again—hopefully to all eyes this time—they could see the ground breaking open and creatures coming through, snarling and biting.

"That was a close call, way too close for comfort!" said Rajan, not quite keeping the strain out of his voice.

"Yes, it was!" Elderanna replied. "It was enough excitement for a year for me, I do not need any more of that kind!" Putting both arms around her up there in the air, Rajan made it clear that he felt the same way. Drifting along the side of the mountain, they decided to go on for the night as the stars were out. That way they would escape any pursuers, scouts or spies that were out looking for them. Sailing through the night air, they put many miles between themselves and any would-be pursuers before touching back down again and going to sleep. But Elderanna had to put strong protective measures along the perimeter around their camp before Rajan allowed himself to relax and settle down for what remained of the night.

As all mornings, Rajan woke early, but this time he thought his internal watch had fooled him. It was still dark, as dark as the middle of the night, and no stars were to be seen. He touched Elderanna's shoulder and whispered, "Something has happened to the stars, there is no light in the sky, not even the moon."

Elderanna, who was after all tired after their ordeal the night before, opened her eyes and sat up. "What are you talking about?" she asked.

"Look," said Rajan. "There are no stars and there is no moon. It is the darkest night I have ever experienced; it is so dark I cannot even see my hand in front of my eyes!" This was true, she found out, and as she tried to look around her, she also saw that the only things she could see, was Rajan—who was sitting next to her—and the faint glow from the fire.

What on earth could have happened? Even clouds could not be as dense as this?

At roughly the same time, Mojastic was also studying the night sky, looking for stars or a ray of moonlight, but in vain. He had woken many hours before Rajan, having had the worst nightmare of all times, but one he remembered very little of, and had witnessed the darkening of the night sky, the stars being extinguished one by one until the skies above him was completely black. It fit with the mood he was in after the nightmare. It had not yet relinquished his grip on him, and he found himself sweating uncontrollably at the thought of it. His dream had started out being just that; glimpses of his daily life in the castle, with a smiling and loving Myra at his side, but then it had changed, slowly, the way the worst nightmares do. Myra had gone from loving to scheming and frigid cold, without her outward appearance changing at all, tools that he used each day suddenly appeared to actively try to kill or maim him, and when he raced to get his son in his crib, all he found was a rotting corpse leering at him...the rest of the nightmare had been mercifully erased from his memory.

Cautiously, he got up. One of the disadvantages of being in the dark was the loss of balance. *You do not know how much you rely on your visual capabilities before they do not work anymore,* he thought to himself. Staring into the darkness proved to no avail; pitch black did not even begin to describe the blackness that surrounded him. Feeling panic beginning to play along his spine, he forced himself to calm down and think for a moment, *What can I do that will be of service to me in this situation, but will not alert any beings or creatures to my presence?* Relaxing his mind, he felt himself slowly sinking into his brain through layer after layer of consciousness. Finally, he connected to his core, where the seat of his magic capabilities was placed. Mojastic knew that he was vulnerable in this state. If an enemy should happen to come across him, he would be dead meat—as simple as that, as he would not have time enough to recover himself before the attack. But if he wanted to go on, this was his only option, "and that is the end of my discussion!" he said to himself.

Fortunately, no one came along, and he was able to re-animate a while later. He had found the answer he had been searching for, now was the time to see if he could execute the trick—if he had the skill to do so. He stared into the darkness, searching not for visible signs of life, but for the energy-threads that passing life forms left behind in their wake. And it came to him, slowly, the whole surrounding area was lit up in a multitude of colours. Mostly greens of varying hues, together with shades of blue, orange, yellow, and brown, covered the landscape and showed a different aspect of its life. But it also lit up his surroundings in a way that made it possible to keep travelling on, displaying the features of rock, sand and clay, and making the distance to the ground measurable to him when flying. Soon, he was in the air again, feeling the cool air on his face.

At the same time, Elderanna was concluding a similar exercise, and standing up she said to Rajan, "This is one of those moments when it is easier to do than to explain." She then reached up and touched his forehead gently, pressing her index finger just a little bit against him. He sensed that something was about to change in his head but found that he trusted her completely and allowed himself to just let go.

Closing his eyes, he could feel himself swimming as it were in a warm, comfortable fluid—like a baby—and when he emerged from it, he knew he had been altered forever. Now opening his eyes, he found that he could see, but like Mojastic, he saw things, shapes, and colours in a way—and in wavelengths—he never had before. Still marvelling over his new-born power of sight, he helped Elderanna pack up their camp and made ready for another day of flying. "When do you think we will be there?" he asked into the air.

Elderanna smiled, "Well, now who is sounding like a little pup? We will get there when we do, and that is all I can say." That being said, they resumed their journey.

As the hours went by, the mountain became increasingly uneasy, slowly lighting up the sky with an eerie orange sheen. Rumblings from its depths spoke of tremors deep within, and the shaking now sometimes also came to the surface, like bubbles in a bottle. The light shining from its craters shone brighter, and at the same time more ferociously—as if it was bubbling with anger and about to burst.

A sudden crack was heard, and everyone in the immediate area next to the volcano looked up in suspense. Sparks were flying from the summit, or so it seemed, but it soon became evident that it was more than sparks raining down from the crater. Boulder after boulder threatened the three gliding warriors and they had to increase their altitude significantly to avoid them. From their vantage point in the sky, they could see what had hitherto been hidden from them as creature after creature made its way to safety. The volcano, which initially looked like a fireworks-show, now looked more and more deadly and unstable, and if they had known somewhere where they would be safe, they would have escaped tither as fast as they could. That was sadly not the case, so they had to wait it out in the relative safety of the higher altitudes.

Lightning had also begun to strike, and as it were thunderbolts with a lot of energy in them, the situation was beginning to take its toll on all three of them. The lightning flashed by them at such speeds that all they left behind was the smell of burnt air and gases. It was a frightening situation and it got worse. With an ear-splitting thunderous roar, the air itself was cleaved in many pieces, tearing Elderanna and Rajan apart, and sending Mojastic, half conscious, tumbling to the ground. When the other two landed—hard—on the surface, they found it altered in a very scary way, the lightning stroke had burnt the sand, making a giant window in the crust, so they could see into the underground—without any elaidaring or Sinestral involved—but that meant that the beings in the underground could also look out—and see them.

One of the many who were standing in the tunnels at that moment, was Kerrsh; the hooded figure who had given Mojastic food and water during their meeting the day before. Now, he was standing, looking up at Rajan and blinking in surprise, another man? And just like the first man, there seemed to be magic in this one too, but not nearly as much, he concluded. He was just about to turn around and give orders for this man's capture, when something else caught his eye. Turning back, he could see what resembled a star behind this man, a star with bright, white, warm light, only a thousand times stronger than any star he had ever seen. Curious and a little frightened, he walked forward a few steps and was left open-mouthed for at least a minute. It could not be!!! She could not exist; she had been banned and thrown away. But still…? At that moment, the star stepped in front of the man and everything went white. Running for cover, all he could think, was, *If she is still alive, then perhaps what we have been told is not entirely true…???* And on the heels of that thought, *But can I—or we—trust her?*

Chapter 18
The Calling of the King

Mojastic got to his knees, head ringing from the impact, trying to get his bearings. He could see, as through a fog, the contours of creatures running in all directions, scared out of their wits by the lightning and thunder that had been unleashed. Getting shakily to his feet, his first thought was to find cover, but looking around, he was unable to discover any shelter in his surroundings. Putting his feet firmly under himself, he began to run toward the mountainside, looking for cover there. When he got close enough, he could see many crags and crannies, but none big enough for a full-grown man. However, he discovered a crack in the ground, and without thinking twice—perhaps not even once—he jumped down into the caves underneath him. Immediately, he was filled with a sense of panic; chimes, bells, and wind-flutes were sounding, together with drums and gongs, making it a cacophony worse that he had ever heard. For a split second, he feared he was going to go deaf due to all the noise. Then it stopped, as suddenly as it had begun, and instead he could now hear grinding sounds like a huge door creaking or a grinding stone of immense dimensions. The sound was enough to make him loose his foothold with the vibrations it created, and together with the relative darkness down there it gave him a claustrophobic, nightmarish feeling.

As if that was not enough, he began to hallucinate, he was starting to see shadows of a most peculiar kind; elongated and wiry, with claws and fangs. When he began to run to get away from these phantoms, they followed, wailing and howling enough to make his blood run cold. The caverns in which he was running did not keep a straight line, they wound their way along, splitting sometimes in two, sometimes in three, and folding back on themselves, making it close to impossible to know where he was or was going. After some turns, he became aware that he could not hear the shadows anymore, but he kept at it anyway. He ran in the darkness for some time, not knowing what he was doing, and he had just given himself a scolding for not paying attention to his whereabouts when he heard an echo ahead. Acting on pure instinct he threw himself down and narrowly escaped a fall that would have meant his certain demise. There, just inches from his toes, was a void of unknowable size and depth. He could not sense its boundaries, it felt like he was on the edge of night itself, but he could hear something? He strained his ears to hear what it was and recoiled quickly from the edge when he heard his name being whispered from the depths. "Mojastic… Mojastic…Mojastic…" It sounded like an echo from far away, but he was aware by now that everything was not as it seemed in this underground world.

In the end, he did what he saw as his only option; he answered the call. In response, the void filled with scorching flames and it was all he could do to avoid catching fire. Turning around on his heels, he was on the run again, cursing himself for being reckless and hasty.

Rajan was stumbling along without seeing much. The lightning storm had died down a bit and the mountain had quieted, but it was still restless. All about him was rubble and rocks, thrown around by the ejections of mass from the crater, and some of those stones were hot! He should know, he had nearly stepped on some of them. If only he could find Elderanna! She had been there with him, but then there had been an explosion from the mountain, and she had stepped in front of him to shield him, and that was all he could remember. He came to himself lying on the ground, with pebbles lying all over him, but unhurt. All was quiet, there was nothing to hear or sense around him, and even with his new powers of vision he could not see anything. He was beginning to fear that this time he had lost her for good, when he heard her voice from over a small ridge. Scurrying up as quickly as he could, he came to the top and was met with an astounding sight. In the little hollow between two ridges, he could see two white shapes, one small and one large. There was something familiar with the small one, he was sure it would have to be Elderanna, but she was shining! And the large…was a dragon! White it was, as if it was made of snow and starshine, and illuminated from within the same way a star would be, or so he imagined. It bent its long, graceful neck to her, and allowed her to scratch it behind the ears…

That is that! he thought, *I am going crazy!*

"No, you are not, Rajan!" came the answer from down in the hollow. "You are seeing this, and if you join us, I will introduce you!" On unsteady feet he made his way down to them and was introduced to the dragon.

"Rajan, this is Boreala, my steed of old." Shocked and bewildered, he almost curtseyed to it, but caught himself just in time and bowed instead.

"Boreala, this is Rajan, my beloved." Taken aback by her words, he just stared at her while Boreala nodded graciously to him, and he could have sworn, hid a smile. Elderanna took his hand and led him a little to the side.

"I have something to tell you, my dear," she began. Rajan looked into her radiant eyes and felt like a flock of butterflies had just taken off from his stomach. "When we fell to the ground, just before we landed, I suddenly remembered. I remembered who I was, and what I was, and the truth is both, exhilarating and frightening. Now, I have got to tell you the story of how I became Elderanna, and then we must decide what we shall do."

Rajan had been dumbfounded during her speech, but now he found he could speak again, and before he knew what he was going to say, he had said what was in his heart, "Wait just one second! Before you tell me anything, I have something I should have told you eons ago." The way he held her, putting both arms around her and looking straight into her face, made her breathless and dizzy, and then he continued, "I love you, Elderanna or whoever you are! I love you to the sun and back again, and I will follow you into a star if that is what I must do to be with you. Life has no meaning without you, and death does not bother me as long as I know you are with me!" and then he kissed her to the applause of Boreala, who was really smiling now.

When she freed herself from his kiss, Elderanna was smiling radiantly, and touched his face gently with her hands. "I know," she said simply, "and the feeling you have for me is only matched by the feeling I have for you! But now, we have to talk!"

Not many miles away, with his back against the wall, Mojastic had stopped to catch his breath. His lungs were burning in his chest, and his heart was hammering the way a sledgehammer does when wielded by a cunning but ferocious blacksmith. He looked around to seek a way out and found it in a crack that was running the height of the tunnel, just wide enough for a man to sneak through. He was making his way to this crack when he heard his name being spoken behind him. Turning lightning quick, he was not able to see anyone there, but he could sense that something was off. Getting ready to squeeze through the crack, he held still for a second and then said in a commanding tone, using his powers again, "Reveal yourself!" Instantly, creatures and beings of every kind came through the tunnel at full speed, all making straight for him. In a heartbeat, he was through the crack and made his stand with his back against the mountain wall.

Chapter 19
No Quarters Given,
None Taken

It was a battle of which bards would have sung long praises, soldiers would have ranked it as amongst the fiercest ever, and the soft of heart would have cried many a tear. In short, it was epic, and as with so many such battles, no one was there to record it or watch it. But then perhaps that was just as well, for a bard, even one of distinguished accomplishments, could not have hidden the brutality and carnage of the scene.

Wave after wave of incoming creatures, or beasts, or beings—whatever you would call them, it did not mask the fact that they were swarming like ants over the hills, up from the canyons, and over the ridges. All of them were coming straight at him, baring their fangs, bristling with spikes, or lifting their stingers, and all of them in a frenzy of bloodlust, completely mad. Mojastic slowly lifted his eyes to the sky, but no help was coming from that direction. For a moment he looked resigned, then he lifted his arms over his head, and his voice rose like thunder over the mad screeches from the advancing crowd. What happened next was inexplicable, and to his foes, frightening beyond words.

In an instant, a wall of fire, blue, sparkling fire, was erected between him and his assailants. It crackled and spit, looking electrical in substance, and it had a devastating effect on the beings that touched it or in any way tried to breach it. One after another, they had a go, and one after another they disappeared in blue flames whilst throwing off sparks like a fireworks display. The wall was in fact more of a box than a wall, covering him from every conceivable angle, even from underground attacks. This wall, or box, held his foes at bay, not permitting a single attacker to find his or her way in to the lone wizard standing inside it, but as with all kinds of wizardry it took a toll on the wielder of the spell.

Mojastic felt it draining his powers, slowly but surely, and he knew that sooner or later he would be forced to bring out an attacking spell to combat the army of beasts. The problem was that he was completely new to this game and did not feel certain of his talents. Yes, he had mastered elaidaring almost effortlessly once he tried it, as well as sinestraling, spellcasting, and to some extent foretelling. But to use his abilities as weapons? That was a long step out of his comfort range, although 'comfort range' might not be a fitting description of the situation. *You are a fool!* he thought to himself. *Get over yourself and do or die, those are your choices!*

With that encouraging thought, he threw an explosive spell out into the throng in front of him, with the result that all of them went scrambling for cover, squealing in fright. After that he kept dropping bomb after bomb into their midst, and it did work well on the waves of incoming enemies; their ranks were thinning visibly. *But not enough,* he thought to himself. Trying another kind of spell, throwing lightning bolts at specific creatures, had a solid effect on the crowd for a while, but still they kept coming at him, though fewer than before. He kept switching between the two spells of attack, but he could feel his powers waning fast and there was no end to the foes in sight.

His newfound abilities needed practise to reach their promise, and he had not had time for any practising or learning of spells—the adversary had seen to that. With a pang, he remembered Myra, standing in the moonlight, rejoicing in the fact that he was a spellcaster also, and dreaming of the things they would do together when this ordeal was over. That would not happen now, he knew, and it hurt so bad that for a moment he thought he was going to lay down and give up. In the end, however, he decided to get justice for Myra, and the only way to get that, was by confronting that cursed sorcerer, Rhanddemarr! Thinking that, he turned his full attention to the present situation.

He would have to think along different lines, this was going nowhere fast. Looking around him, he saw a path of some sorts in the mountainside. *For goats, most likely, but it will have to do,* he thought to himself. Hastily laying a plan of escape from the frozen situation he was in, he kept his attackers at arm's length, while he got ready for the attempt. Throwing a blinding explosion in front of him, he somersaulted backwards and landed on the ledge he had observed in the mountainside. The ledge ran in an eastward direction, and as he raced toward the direction of the sunrise. He could see faint lines of light begin to appear over the horizon in the east. But it was not enough, and as he well knew, these beings were used to fighting in daylight as well as at night. In front of him, there suddenly rose the mouth of a cave, tall and narrow, but bigger than the ones he had entered before. Without thinking at all, he plunged into the dark and disappeared.

Chapter 20
Into the Deep

He was racing along in the tunnels, trying desperately to find an exit close to the surface, but ending up going deeper instead. It was like the recurring nightmare, something he had dreamed a thousand times before, going into a cave and then just going deeper and deeper, except this time it was for real. If he had thought he was lost in his first visit to the caves that had been only a precursor to this. The network of caves and tunnels seemed to grow while he ran, making it impossible to remember or backtrack his route, and it was so intricate that finding some plan of its layout was nothing but a vanishing dream. He had half expected these tunnels to be filled with fumes and filth, but this was not the case; they gave the impression of being much used for transportation and well kept. The only problem he could identify so far, was that they were warmer than he thought they would be—some of them much warmer.

In order to find his way, he tried out the way-finder spell again, and it worked. He threw it in front of him and it lit up the path as he ran, but it also lit up the spectacles he raced by. Some of these were shaped by the same forces that had made the tunnels and caves in the first place, lava and gases from the volcano, whereas others were beings that had been left behind as guards. He could see their shocked countenances when he approached them, but fortunately the experience of seeing him, left them dumbfounded and unable to stop him when he sped past them.

At long last, he was unable to go any further without some rest, and he stopped at a crossroads of kind to catch his breath, leaning heavily against the tunnel wall and drawing air in raw, heaving gasps. Dimly, he became aware of movement below his field of vision, and looking down he saw an army of…little furry balls? He stared in surprise, what in the world could these things be? They came swarming up from the tunnel to the left, which he slowly realised must be one leading under the volcano and assailed him where he stood. At first, he thought that the little fur balls did not present any danger to him, but when they tried to carry him away, he protested. His protests did not help much, and when he tried to shrug them off, they reacted by biting his hands with little, sharp teeth. Throwing him off balance, he was efficiently thrown to the ground and landed on a furry carpet made up of the little creatures, all keeping close together. Down there, he could hear them chirping and chattering among themselves with small bird-like voices. He found to his surprise that they did not sound evil or malignant at all, the impression he got was one of friendliness and urgency.

The carpet on which he was carried made its way into the tunnel to the left and sped along, giving him the confusing feeling of being on a magic carpet ride through the air. He was still trying to get up, but the ride was so fast, and the road so filled with turns and bumps that it was no easy feat to do so. Suddenly, one of the fur balls jumped up on his chest and approached his head. Standing just a few inches from his face, he heard the creature speak in his own tongue, and tongue-tied with shock, he listened to what the little thing had to say.

"We hail you, king of the forest land, and apologise for the way in which we approached you, but there was a bad thing lying in wait for you just down the tunnel from where you stood and we had to get you away before it attacked."

To say that Mojastic was surprised would be the understatement of the year! Then the fur-ball continued, "We wish to bring you toward your goal and keep you safe at the same time, at least as safe as circumstances will allow, and perhaps you will reach your goal and achieve your purpose. If you do that you will also help many people of which you know nothing, but who will be forever grateful to you. Will you accept our humble help?"

Thinking to himself that he really did not have many, or any, options, Mojastic nodded. "I thank you for your kind offer and accept your help with a grateful heart," he answered. Looking relieved, the fur-ball turned to his companions and cried out some orders in his own language, and intended to leave, but Mojastic stopped him. "Before you go, tell me what you call yourselves," he said, "it is only right that I should know the kind of my saviours."

The fur-ball beamed up at him, or at least that was the impression he got, and then said, "We are the Chaiga, and my name is Illiot and I am a chief."

"My regards to you, Illiot," Mojastic replied, "and my deepest gratitude to all Chaigas for securing my getaway!" Bowing to Mojastic, Illiot turned and disappeared back into the throng of Chaigas transporting him into the dark.

At last they came to a cavernous hall of an unfathomable size. They were now deeper than he could have imagined the caves to go, beyond anything, he had read about or heard about before, and the hall they had entered was big beyond belief. He could not see the walls, even with his way-finder light, and when he tried to whistle, the only sound was echoes and even those were long in coming back. When he strained his eyes however, he could see an orange light, in shape not unlike the Chaiga, bobbing gently in what he assumed was the middle of the hall. Getting to his feet at last, he stood and contemplated it for a while. Approaching it with care, he became aware that the Chaiga were no longer with him. Where they had gone, and why they had gone, he did not know, but he presumed it had to do with the orange ball of light. Perhaps it was their deity or an oracle of some kind? Either way he was now on his own once again, and the only company he had, was this light. It seemed to be moving gently, but there was no breeze that he was aware of. It could be that the light was a part of a construction that he could not see, but when he got closer, he saw that the light was in fact floating serenely in mid-air, unrestrained by any structure or device.

Having reached the light he did not know what to do, so in the end he sat down with the light-ball in front of him and just studied it, floating in front of his eyes.

Chapter 21
Hidden Questions, Forgotten Answers

The moment stretched into infinity while his limbs slowly regained their strength and his mental faculties threw off the fatigue that had plagued them since his flight into the cave system began. Staring into the light, he became aware that he was going into a meditative state, loosing track of time and place, just floating along with it. It was a peaceful state of mind, one that did more for charging his powers than anything else he could have tried. Suddenly he became aware that the light was changing colour from orange to red and then green. As the colours kept changing and the globe kept bobbing gently, he heard a voice inside his head, "Ask!" What? What was he supposed to ask? He thought for a moment, then said, "What do you want me to ask?"

"What do you need answered?" came the reply.

"I need to know how to beat my adversary," he said.

"Is that what you need or what you want?" the light then asked in return. And thus, it went on, one question followed by another, and answered by new questions till he felt exhausted. He did not get any of the answers he had been hoping for when the exchange began, only new questions, and at first this tired him thoroughly in addition to making him irritated. But then, he remembered a tale that Elderanna had told him, of the man with a thousand questions. In that tale, the questions were a means of making the asker think out the answers for himself. At the time he had thought the tale a tedious way of making a philosophical point, but now he was not so sure, perhaps there was something in it after all?

With that in mind he went back to one of his first questions, the one about what he needed, and asked simply, "Where is the love of my life now?"

A silence fell in the hall, then the light replied, "Her essence is in the air, in the water, in the soil, and in all life around you. Never far from you and her son."

He gasped and drew air, almost losing his grip on the situation, then tried another question, "Are my two best friends still alive?"

The light bobbed, then answered, "Your two best friends are together, and you will see them in time." This made him sigh with relief, as his thoughts had gone constantly to them and their fate over the last weeks. Now that he had found the key to how this game of riddles should be played, he felt more confident that he could get the answers he needed, but as it turned out, the light was still an enigmatic creature and gave more puzzling answers than straightforward ones. One of the most confusing ones, was the answer he got when he asked who his opponent really was, "Who is the prisoner of birth?" As he had no idea how to interpret that, he let the matter be for now.

In the end, he had only three questions left that were most prominent in his mind, "Will I be able to make the sorcerer pay for his misdeeds? Will I get justice for Myra and all those who have died? Will I ever see my son again?"

The light-ball was silent for a long time, then said, "Listen to your heart."

"What do you mean?" he asked, almost begging for an answer.

"Listen to your heart," it said again, "your heart has the answers already. Listen to your heart!" With that, the light suddenly was extinguished and left him in complete darkness of the densest kind, a darkness so intense it felt almost physical. The sound of silence was total, and the internal sound of his heartbeats sounded like heavy drums in his ears, ominous and deep.

Chapter 22
Lost but Not Alone

He felt lost, as lost as a castaway in the middle of an unknown ocean. Lost—and alone. In this darkness nothing existed except his heartbeat thundering in his ears, growing louder by the second. His sense of direction was stripped from him the moment the light went out, and in this huge hall it was not an easy job to regain. The obvious thing to do would be to use his way-finder spell, but to his astonishment and surprise it did not work. He tried to use echolocation, but due to the sheer size of the hall, he found his ears and the whistles he managed to produce were totally inadequate for the task. Stumbling his way forward, at least the way he had been facing when the darkness fell, he tried to put one foot in front of the other with utmost care, using his hands to feel the air in front of his face in case there should be something in front of him.

Thinking about his situation, he was suddenly filled with an inexplicable sense of mirth, "What if I suddenly put my hand into someone's mouth?" He snickered, but the sound was so distorted and amplified by the echo that he soon laughed no more. Without his spell to light the way, he was reduced to a blind man in a maze... Still he continued forward, half-stumbling, half-shuffling like an old man. As time passed, he realised that the air was growing thick and—in loss of a better word—unbreathable. It had a faint smell of sulphur to it, as well as a tinge of burnt sand. He still could not see anything, but the smells became stronger as he shambled along. How was it possible to feel so isolated and trapped at the same time as he felt adrift and without boundaries?

His breath was beginning to sound harsh and ragged again, as if he had been running for a long time. It was also making an echo, or was it an echo? Stopping suddenly, his heart once again pounding against his ribs, he listened. In the silence that fell, he could hear a soft hiss, or…? He felt fear leap down his throat and start to choke his sanity.

Elderanna was sitting on the soft sand beside Rajan, who was struggling to get his head wrapped around the things she had told him. He had a thousand questions and a million answers that he had no questions for, but the most important reason for his befuddledness was the beautiful creature sitting next to him, radiant and shining. A soft light lay around her, shone from her eyes, and glittered in her hair. It made her seem like a star, or in other words, confirmed the impression Rajan already had of her. His eyes changed subtly from wide-eyed wonder to the soft look they had, whenever he looked at her.

"If you had been the queen of a distant planet, or the goddess of a new religion, I could not have cared less. I love you, no matter what, who, or when you are!" The smile Elderanna gave him at that moment told him all he needed to know. Then she rose to her knees, wrapped his face in her hands and began to sing in a beautiful low voice.

As the song progressed, her voice changed character, from soft and low to rich and vibrant, from low-pitched, almost a harmonious tremor to high-pitched and ringing like a bell. It was a song he had never heard before. The words and the melody were totally unfamiliar and somehow alien to him, but it was the singing that brought tears of joy to his eyes; that angelic voice that just rose to the sky and filled his very existence. When the song took hold of him, he could see images appearing in his vision, images of the story and history she had told him, as well as images of the many possible futures that could lie ahead for them. He saw the birth of this planet, Dragora, how the great mother-dragon had tended to it and how it had flourished in the early years. He saw the awakening of the different species that lived on the planet, coming to life one after the other, and he saw the arrival of two of great power, a woman and a man, sister and brother. Staring wide-eyed into Elderanna's deep eyes he saw the ages unfolding before him and realised how ancient she was.

They rose gently up, swimming among the little sparks that flew off Elderanna, and were soon high up in the air from where he could witness the rest of the song unfolding. It was an ashen world down there, but each little spark that rained down to earth took root and grew rapidly up, stretching toward its origin. And when the blossom opened, memories, each looking like a little star, would unfold from them, memories of Elderanna's past. For the first time in a long time, she accessed her full life-story and Rajan got to experience it together with her. It was an honour and an awe-inspiring moment he would never forget.

For Elderanna, it felt like total freedom and putting her roots in the soils where they belonged at the same time. She almost burst for joy, could barely contain herself in the exhilaration of the moment. But it was not all good memories; in her past she could also see betrayal, and the dark lust of a love gone awry, that of a brother for a sister. It filled her eyes with tears for a moment, but then she acknowledged that a choice is a personal thing, and each person will have to stand for and take responsibility for the choices he or she makes, not only for the actions that follows from those choices. With that thought, she could feel the pang of regret and the pain that it had brought her, finally give way to the new love she had discovered. The light that emanated from her grew in strength until it lit up their whole surroundings with a soft sheen of white brilliance. The last memory was the oldest, and with it came her name as she had been called in ancient times. She sang it out as the memory hit her, Ahroree! I am Ahroree!

Chapter 23
The Tournament
Battle of Kings

Meanwhile, trapped far underground, Mojastic continued his wandering in loneliness, feeling very small and vulnerable. The soft hissing, he had heard or thought he had heard, was now a certainty, and it was steadily growing more audible and insistent in character. It had also risen in pitch, from the low wheezing that was initially, to more of a whining sound, although he could still hear the different levels in between, so perhaps it was more than one creature producing them?

Asking questions can be a dangerous game, especially when you do not know if you want to hear them answered. Mojastic got his answer in a sudden and heart-stopping way; lights suddenly came on and he found himself in a large tunnel, crawling with beasts, creatures and otherworldly-looking beings, or monsters, as a child would call them if they were encountered in a nightmare. Nightmare it was not; this was reality and Mojastic was again running for his life, not knowing if there even existed a way out of this situation. Deeper and deeper the tunnel led him, into the bowels of the earth or so it seemed, and behind him he could hear the wheezing and screeching of a multitude of enemies, clawing their way after him. Far ahead he could see the tunnel bending sharply to the left, and what lay beyond that bend was impossible to say, but as he had no choice it did not really matter. For a moment he felt beside himself, thinking, "There have been so many tunnels lately, I am beginning to think I am a badger!" but the humour lasted only for a split second; the present situation did not inspire laughter, nor did the sight that met him when he turned that bend in the tunnel.

He could not see the walls of the hall he found himself in, for the creatures covering every surface, even the ceiling. The mere numbers of them made him stop for just a fragment of time, but it was enough for the creatures behind him to reach him at last. Desperately, he drew his sword and fought them with a savageness that amounted to an absolute frenzy, but they were too many and, he perceived, organised. A sudden attack from behind toppled him and brought him to his knees, and then he was overpowered, weighted down by huge numbers of foes who all wanted to be the one who vanquished him. Just as he was about to give up, he heard a commanding voice, "Raise him up, but keep his hands behind his back, and remember to take his sword!"

He had heard that voice before, he knew. It was the voice that had rung out from the sky in Arboria, the voice of Rhanddemarr, the sage, the voice of a despot and a sorcerer. And there he was in the flesh, standing about six feet tall, he was by no means a small man, and he had a strong and well-knit body. His face was cleanshaven, with deep-set, sharp, grey eyes and long, black hair bound together in a tail that ran halfway down his back. Clad in a coat of mail and girded with a sword, he was an intimidating sight. But being pulled to his feet, Mojastic was taller than his opponent by eight inches, as well as more broad-shouldered. Otherwise they seemed remarkably similar; long hair in tail or braid down their backs, sword and mail-coat, and an imposing figure. But their faces and eyes were what told the multitude of creatures surrounding them that they were indeed of vastly different sorts, for Mojastic had a well-kept beard and moustache, and large blue eyes with mirth normally twinkling in their depths.

The cold eyes of Rhanddemarr studied him at length without saying anything, then he obviously thought he had seen enough, for he signalled for Mojastic to be brought to the centre of the hall where the floor was raised. It was a sort of throne room, Mojastic suddenly realised. He could see a stone dais with a solid throne of sorts standing on top, but he also noticed that the throne itself seemed too big for Rhanddemarr when he went to sit down upon it. He wondered briefly if the throne had been intended for someone else but was quickly brought back to the present by his guards' rough handling of him.

"So, you have come here to commit murder," he heard Rhanddemarr say. "Sneak into the land, stealthily and with cruel intentions, a mere vagabond! Look at him!" he called to his congregation. "Look at his untrustworthy, ragged appearance. He is nothing but a thief and an assassin and he will get his just desserts, though not what he came here for!" Mojastic had straightened his back at his first words, and now he stood erect and proud, looking anything but a vagabond. His eyes blazed as he looked up at Rhanddemarr, his fingers clenching and unclenching behind his back. It was a good thing for Rhanddemarr that he was chained up, otherwise that little speech could have had severe consequences for the speaker.

But he would have to endure more in the same vein, for Rhanddemarr went on and on, belittling Mojastic and all that he had with him. He also spoke of the sacrifices made by the people of Dorthnonder; how they had fought bravely for their freedom, and how their martyrdoms would be praised in songs forever. Once this just war was won, they would have access to all that had previously been denied them; vast areas of land and wildlife, theirs for the taking. Mojastic was about to bellow out his thoughts about Rhanddemarr's sanity, when he at last managed to cool down and listen to what he was saying. It was all lying and propaganda, of course, but for what purpose? What was he trying to achieve? Paying attention not only to his wording, but also his body language, and trying to piece the two together with what he already knew about the sorcerer, a sinister picture emerged.

Looking Rhanddemarr in the eyes, Mojastic saw a clever manipulator, immense strength and determination, and a will to rule everything. Perhaps not bad traits in a king if they are modified by compassion and care for the people he rules, but that was not the case here. Mojastic also saw hatred in those eyes, and an extreme cold, more than enough to freeze him solid if he gazed in those eyes for too long. Who was the hatred for? He could not tell. The only thing he was certain of, was that whoever that person might be, he or she would be in boiling waters if Rhanddemarr ever encountered him or her.

He did not get to spend a long time in his reveries—if that was what they could be called—before the present intruded upon him yet again in the form of Rhanddemarr's venomous voice, "So, traitor and spy from the country of Arboria! What have you got to say for yourself that may lessen our sentence?" Mojastic desperately wanted to clear his voice before answering but being afraid that it might be construed as a sign of weakness, he just hoped his voice would not squeak when he gave his answer, "First, I think it would be polite to point out that we knew nothing of your existence before we were under attack. Secondly, as neither I nor any of my counsellors, knew that this country was inhabited, we could not be said to have oppressed anyone living here. Thirdly, it is a bit rich, do you not think, to be talking of planned murder, when you are responsible for the deaths of many people whom I loved, my queen first among them."

Rhanddemarr appeared to be choking on something; his face was pale with livid, red blotches on his cheeks, and his throat and mouth were working furiously, but no sound emerged from those thin lips. When at length he spoke, he was fuming with anger, "Liar! You, whoreson! You will be fodder for the mother, fanning her flames when her slow-running lava kisses the soles of your feet! Take him to the gift-chamber!" With that, he spun around and marched out of the hall at the head of his subjects as they trailed out behind. Mojastic was struggling against his chains but to no avail; all he could do was follow his guards. When they dragged him along, his mind wandered again—perhaps to avoid thinking about what lay in store for him—and he thought of the question-and-answer session he had had with the ball of light in the huge hall.

One of the questions he had not been able to answer when it was asked, was, "Who is the prisoner of birth?" At the time he had thought the answer was 'everybody,' thinking that fate ruled them all and you were bound by the circumstances of your birth, but now, he suddenly realised that he had been wrong. The prisoner of birth was the one who could not cast off the chains that he was born into, the one who did not openly oppose fate and its grip on his reality. A person who could not let anything go, because it was ordained so. A person who was fate's hostage. And then he knew what Rhanddemarr's soliloquy had been about: he firmly thought that he was to be ruler over everything that Dragora contained because fate had said so, and he could not let that go, even if it ruined everything that he wanted to rule. It was almost—but not quite—enough to make him feel sorry on Rhanddemarr's behalf.

The tunnel sloped down quite steeply, and it wound its way deeper and deeper, but at last it reached the point where it levelled off. There, in the middle of the chamber they entered, was a circular hole in the floor with a stone pillar in the centre of it. The stench that rose from the hole was unbelievable, sulphur—strong and pungent, enough to send a man reeling or make him faint. A small stone-bridge ran over the opening onto the central pillar, where a metal pole with chains on it was embedded in the stone, high enough to chain a man much taller than Mojastic to it. There were some remains hanging from the chains, and Mojastic realised he knew whose, Arcull! A grand ring on the middle finger of the hand that was left behind, told the tale of his ending—a brutal one. The smirk on Rhanddemarr's face told Mojastic that he had seen both the discovery and the reaction to it. Then his guards brought him over the bridge and chained him to the pole, before they hurried back to the other side. Standing there with his hands secured over his head, Mojastic stared stoically over at Rhanddemarr, who stood opposite him, leering and smiling coldly, "Well, here our ways will part, I am afraid, but do not worry, you will not have to wait for too long!"

"So, you have more pressing things to attend to, now that you think I am vanquished." Mojastic replied, thinking he could at least try to throw his opponent off balance. It worked even better than he had expected.

"What are you talking about? Are you going to learn how to dissipate and vaporise up from this chamber?" Rhanddemarr and most of his followers were bellowing with laughter.

"What if I am?" Mojastic said. "What if I use my powers and unlock these chains, then summon my sword, seek you out, and finish what I came here for when you feel at ease because you think I am done for?"

"What powers?" asked Rhanddemarr. "Is it that witch that has convinced you that you have powers? Has she turned your head so completely that you believe it yourself? Then this is going to be even more entertaining!" But something in his voice had lost its conviction.

Mojastic could clearly see that the seed of doubt had been sown and was taking root, and he did not waste any time pursuing his advantage, "By all means, go. Take your followers with you and leave me alone down here. Perhaps we will meet again? I will do my best to give you a good fight!"

As if on cue, a person—tall and gangly—in the crowd behind Rhanddemarr quietly approached him and whispered something in his ear. Rhanddemarr looked thoughtful for a moment, then nodded slowly while a smile spread across his face. It was not a pleasant smile, it was cruel and cold, but to Mojastic it was still beautiful; his ruse had worked!

Rhanddemarr had taken the bait and now all bets were off! The guards scurried across the bridge and freed Mojastic from his chains, then hurried back to safe ground again. As the mountain rumbled deep throated below their feet, Mojastic made his way over the bridge and stopped in front of Rhanddemarr.

They stood there for what seemed like an age, staring into each other's eyes. When at last Mojastic spoke, he felt like he had been subject to an interrogation but had gotten off without giving away vital information. "I have one last request," he said. "It is the law in other lands that when someone is accused of treason or similar crimes, he will get a chance to prove his innocence in combat. If he cannot fight for himself, he may appoint a man to do it for him. Will you extend me the courtesy of letting me fight to prove that I am not guilty?" Rhanddemarr stood silent for a second, then looked around at the crowd, assessing them one by one for this unexpected task. Mojastic could nearly see the wheels of his mind turning as he tried them on for size and found them lacking, one after the other. Minutes stretched into eternity while they all waited for Rhanddemarr to speak. When he did so, turning back to face Mojastic, he said acidly, "And what opponent did you have in mind, a Chaiga?"

The crowd roared with laughter, but silence ensued when Mojastic started laughing along with them, "Oh, no, I am on good terms with the Chaiga," he said, "I was thinking more along the lines of a Greitsch, perhaps, or a Daemoin. We have met up with some of those along the way."

"No," said Rhanddemarr, "you are trying to goad us into giving you an opponent you will get the better of. But I will give you one that will be your match and more! You will fight...me! Combat to the death, without weapons; how does that sound?" He stared triumphantly at Mojastic, gloating at what he perceived as an expression of shock on Mojastic's face. It was in fact a look of shock; shock that his opponent had fallen so easily into his trap. Not that it was much of a trap, more a ditch, but he had a chance, and a chance, however slim, was what he had hoped for.

"Challenge accepted," he nodded. "What are the rules?"

"No weapons of any kind, except our powers and abilities, such as they be."

He snickered a little at that, clearly thinking that his powers would outstrip Mojastic's in the blink of an eye. "The combat will continue until one of us is dead, and the survivor will have gained his life and freedom. Understood?"

Mojastic just nodded. "When do we begin?" he asked.

"NOW!" Rhanddemarr screamed, and nearly ended the combat there and then with a thunderbolt singeing Mojastic's hair and left ear. Without thinking, he sent a bolt of electricity back at Rhanddemarr, and then the fight was begun.

Chapter 24
A Prize for a King

Once again, an epic battle had commenced, but this time it had an audience: the crowd that had been standing behind Rhanddemarr had initially run for cover when the first thunderbolt struck out, but now they were peeping from every crack and crevasse in the hall, following the strikes as the fight went on. Rhanddemarr was taken totally by surprise by his intended victim's abilities. He had thought that it would be an easy win, now he had to rethink his strategy in the middle of battle. As the lightning, electrical storms, thunderbolts, and other tools of a sorcerer filled the air with the arid smell of burnt gases and rock, the mountain answered to Rhanddemarr's mood-swings. Rumblings and harsh explosions sounded from the deeps, and an orange light was beginning to glow from the many channels that went down into the bowels of the volcano.

Suddenly, Rhanddemarr uplifted his voice in what resembled a birdcall. In response to his call, a winged steed appeared, Daictyl. It was a sight that inspired fear in anyone who saw it, for it did not resemble any living creature that Mojastic knew from before. It had a toothy beak with fangs, a long—almost elongated—body reminiscent of a snake, huge bat-like wings, and tiny feet, at least twenty of them, underneath its scaly bottom, all with a sharp talon at the end of them. Rhanddemarr leapt from the raised stone-perch where he had been taking cover and landed on Daictyl's back. In response, the beast screamed a high-pitched wail that sent shivers down Mojastic's spine. He did not wait to see how the beast would attack, he did the only sensible thing; slid through a crack in the wall and fled.

As he raced through the tunnels yet again, he almost laughed in his desperation, "Cave-exploring with the king of the forest land, wonderful idea!" There was a ring of, 'been there, done that' to this exercise! But at present, he thought his chances of getting out alive had never been slimmer. What made matters worse was the sudden appearance of obstacles along his path; rock fissures that suddenly opened under his feet, monoliths that turned up unexpectedly, sending him reeling before he regained his balance, and beasts lying in wait for him, where there had been only pebbles a moment earlier. He suspected Rhanddemarr was behind most of these occurrences but had no time for investigation. Turning yet another corner, he found himself face to face with Daictyl, and only a lightning quick reaction saved him from becoming Daictyl's next meal.

When he ran from his enemy once again, he suddenly found himself at the bottom of what seemed like a staircase running up through the rock. He started up, not stopping to catch his breath, and ran as fast as he could upwards. This had to lead him toward the surface, and that was where he wanted to be, in the free air. He almost slipped off the staircase on several occasions, as huge halls and lofty drops opened on either side of the stairs. Rhandemarr on Daictyl was never far away, but Mojastic managed to stay ahead of them, just barely.

But running like this—at full steep flights of that are both unknown and treacherous—has its own dangers, and suddenly his feet touched only empty air. As he fell, he only had time for thinking, *What the...* before two things happened simultaneously: One, he heard Rhanddemarr's insane laughter filling his ears, and two, some huge being picked him unceremoniously out of the air and threw him over its head so that he landed on its back. Then he heard a voice—low and melodious—say, "Hold on tight, it is going to be a bumpy ride!"

First, he and his steed—the white and shining Boreala— charged Rhanddemarr and Daictyl and almost sent them crashing. However, they regained their balance and charged in return, making the Boreala swerve to avoid them and almost toppling Mojastic. They kept at this for a while, steadily driving Rhanddemarr back, but having to dive whenever his attacks came too close for comfort. The two sorcerers threw their curses at each other and dove out of the way all at a blinding speed, so anyone watching would have been totally confused and blinded by the flashes and thunderous bangs. Then Boreala spoke again, "This is getting us nowhere fast, and there are places you have to be and things you will have to do, so the best course for us now is to exit this fray!"

Without further talk, the creature sped along the staircase so fast that the stairs became a blur and the halls and caverns they passed on their way were gone before he could register them. Hanging on for his life, he could only watch as the tunnel suddenly bent again, and open air flowed around his face. Then, Boreala abruptly touched down and arched her back, sending Mojastic sliding to the ground. Landing on his feet, he thanked his saviour for all she had done and then looked around to pinpoint his direction and next move. By now they were far up the side of Mount Dorth, on the high eastern spur of the mountain. Peaks were visible to either side of them, but it was evident that the one they were on continued upwards. He noticed another stair in the mountainside, not far from where they were standing, and looked inquiringly at her. "Yes" came the answer, "that is where your road lies; up to the stars."

For the first time he noticed that she was speaking in his head, not with a voice, but before he could ask her anymore, she had taken wing and was far up in the air, heading south on an errand he could only guess at. Having caught his breath and rested while she had flown him up here, he now started on a new leg of his journey, running up the mountainside. "Thank fate we are already high up, or this would have taken a week!" was his thought when he started running. As he picked up speed and raced up the stairs, they bent out of sight just in time, as Rhanddemarr and his steed exited the channel and started to search for his prey.

Chapter 25
The Last Stand

It felt like he was running up a stair that just kept on getting longer and longer, without him moving upward at all. Endless, like the universe he was heading for, for it really felt like he was running to the stars, into the black night sky. Of course, he knew that it was an illusion, but it was a powerful one and one that stuck with him on his way. It felt like he had been running for ages, when out of the blue Boreala re-appeared, greeting him with a low-pitched and melodious, "Hello again!" This time she did not have to pick him up, he jumped from the mountainside onto her back with an agile leap, greeting her warmly as he landed.

And it was not a moment too soon: out of the low-lying cloud-cover Daictyl with its rider appeared, speeding toward them. Boreala did not have to tell him to hang on, he clung to her back with a firm grip of his hands and thighs, bending close to her neck as she flew straight up. The speed with which she flew was exhilarating and heart stopping, and her direction was straight out into the great void. Daictyl had no chance of following her, she was outdoing it in both speed and height. Up there they could see the whole world under them, laid out like a map but so much clearer and in more detail than he could ever have imagined. On the edge of the great void—the universe—he could see the sun as it approached morning on his side of the planet, and the awe that this sight inspired in him, left him speechless.

But being up here for too long was not an option; they would both either freeze to death or suffocate, or Mojastic would, anyway. So, they dove back down through the tempestuous clouds covering the mountaintop. Crashing through the cloud cover, closely followed by Rhanddemarr, Mojastic jumped from the back of Boreala and landed on a natural platform at the very summit. Rhanddemarr also jumped from his steed, and landed a little to the side of Mojastic, firing his curses before he had even landed. Mojastic countered with another curse, and so they were at it again, blasting curses and bolts of lightning at each other without one of them getting the upper hand.

While the combat was at its most intense, Mojastic became aware of a bright light—almost like a twin sun—coming down from a great height, heading their way. Being momentarily thrown off his guard by this, he felt his hair stand on end as Rhanddemarr very nearly hit the mark with a bolt of lightning. The next moment he was also staring at the twin sun descending rapidly toward them, but as opposed to Mojastic, he seemed to recognise it for what it was: two people together, floating on the winds of the upper atmosphere, shining so brightly it hurt their eyes to look directly at them. When they got closer, he could see that they were riding in a sort of orb or globe. He also recognised the brightest of them, realising with a shock that he not only knew who it was but knew the person very well: it was Elderanna!

But it was Rhanddemarr's reactions that took most of his focus.

Mojastic could only stare at Rhanddemarr while his face underwent the strangest contortions—almost like a mirror-image in a pond with ripples—and rage and hatred gushed forth in a flood. It became clear who the hatred was for that Mojastic had sensed in that deep hall: Elderanna. But the name Rhanddemarr used was Ahroree, an unfamiliar name to Mojastic, but very fitting to her, although he could not explain why. Rhanddemarr was screaming curses, throwing spells and behaving like a lunatic, without any of that making any marks or impact on Ahroree. Her companion, Mojastic realised, was none other than Rajan. But he was greatly changed since Mojastic had last seen him. Now he looked younger, healthier, stronger, and more strapping than ever before.

By now, Rhanddemarr had positioned himself on the very summit of Mount Dorth, screaming wildly in his rage, while Ahroree fended off his attacks almost as if they were flies on a summer afternoon. This in turn made Rhanddemarr even angrier, and Mojastic began to wonder if it was possible to burst with anger. But at last he realised that if he wanted Rhanddemarr gone, he would have to do it himself, for it dawned on him that perhaps Ahroree was just as powerless to harm Rhanddemarr as he was powerless to harm her, regardless of his rage. He would have to ask her afterward if that was the case. Straightening up, he positioned himself and hoped that Rhanddemarr would not sense what he was doing until it was too late. He raised his hands over his head, and began to sing an ancient spell, one that he had encountered when they were searching for countermeasures in the eldest books, but which he did not understand the use for, until this very moment.

Gently swaying to and from, he could sense the mountain answering with a low rumble under his feet, one that swelled rapidly as he called the mountain and its force for good, as a life-giver, not a life-taker, and a re-newer instead of a destroyer. It rose to a great roar, and Rhanddemarr became aware that something was happening at last, but his rage and his focus on Ahroree made him too slow to react. Still, he had a moment of sanity just before the lava-jet erupted from the summit, exactly where he stood. Turning his face toward Mojastic, he looked shocked and disbelieving, but Mojastic swore later that he could also see a measure of relief in that look. Then the lava broke through, and sending its stream out into space, Rhanddemarr went with it, burning like a torch in greeting of the sunrise.

At that moment the twin sun set off a shower of stars that covered the ground around the mountain for many miles, and a song of life burst from Mojastic's lips as he rejoiced when the sun's rays hit him on the face. He was joined by Ahroree and Rajan, and the three voices blended their melodies together, weaving in and out of each other like a work of filigree. When the sun rose over the horizon at last, spreading its light over the landscape beneath, the three friends met for the last time. Mojastic could not, at first, take his eyes off Rajan; the change in the man was formidable! And it was not only the exterior that had changed, something in the fabric of his being had been released, something hidden there his whole life. *Is this what true love can do to a person?* he wondered.

Ahroree heard his question without him saying anything, "Dear friend, life holds many surprises for a man who walks with his eyes open!" Then she kissed him on the cheeks and held his hands for a second. After her goodbye, Rajan stepped in and gave Mojastic a warm embrace before joining Ahroree in her glowing orb, "We will be seeing you, although you might not see us!" And then the globe exploded into a million stars and they were gone.

Mojastic was left alone on the peak while the sun rose over the horizon and the mountain's tremor subsided. He sighed; it was a long way down, but then again, it is the job that does not get started that takes the longest to finish! With that, he strode to the edge of the mountain, found the stairs, and started the long climb down. He was followed by a ray of light and—he thought he could almost hear it—faint ethereal music that kept him company through the mists and fog lying on the mountainside.

Walking on foot down the whole way took him several days, even more than was needed for the walk itself, for he used his time well. Healing his inner scars and closing the wounds was a long process, but he felt that he had gotten off to a good start by the time he reached the mountain's roots. Along the way he could see where the stars from the orb had taken root, little, tiny seedlings sprouted everywhere. Minute flowers, miniature trees—that would become giant when fully grown—grass, reeds, and bushes. And where life grows, other life forms will join in, he had seen little birds and small animals already. The whole mountain and its surroundings were filled with budding promise. He felt his mood lighten and allowed himself the luxury of relaxing and letting go of the watchfulness that had been his companion for so long now. However, that might not have been the best idea. Perhaps he had been getting a little too relaxed, because when he reached the foot of the mountain, he could see row after row of creatures waiting for him, many of whom he had had the dubious pleasure of meeting earlier. So, to say that he became a little apprehensive would be a great understatement.

But he was secure in his newfound ability as a sorcerer, and that gave him confidence, so he went forward and greeted the man standing in front. It was only when he got close enough that he recognised the figure. He was the same man who had met him on that misty evening and shared food and water with him! And now that he saw him, he also realised that it was the same figure who had whispered to Rhanddemarr when he was trying to get him to commit to combat! Stepping forward he took the outstretched hand in a firm grip and said, "I am Mojastic, king of Arboria and Afamia. To whom do I have the pleasure of speaking?"

"Kerrsh, king of Nadara, the dual kingdom of Maigarr and Dorthnonder, and forever grateful to you who have freed us from the harsh chains of the dark sorcerer!"

"Then we both owe each other our lives and shall forever live in peace with one another," said Mojastic. He then raised his voice and spoke to all the people of the two parts of the kingdom who were present, "Hear me, all good people of Nadara! From this day, I say that the kingdoms of Nadara and my realm which is the kingdom of Arboria and Afamia, shall live in peace with one another; helping each other in need, celebrating life when we are together, and welcome each other as friend when we visit each other! Hear my pledge of friendship and let this be our bond, forever!"

The cheers and cries of joy was music to his ears, although it had sounded harsh and strange when he had heard it before. It also turned out that Kerrsh was as good as his word: that evening and night was spent sitting next to the fire, talking and philosophising, starting up a strong friendship for the years to come. The next morning Mojastic and his new friend bade each other farewell as he started on his homeward journey—a very different journey from the one who had gotten him there. *Learning to know a stranger, really changes your perspective,* he thought philosophically when he started on the long journey home, the sun thawing the frost that had formed in his heart, as he walked.

Epilogue

When he reached the lands of Afamia at last, he was an altered man. His beard was still auburn, his hair as well, and his eyes still laughed and twinkled. But his physique—always good—was now downright impressive, and he walked with a confidence in his step that had never been so pronounced before. He met up with his remaining general, Trecon, and briefly explained to him what had happened. It was from Trecon he learned that their trouble had ended when he had entered Nadara, for then all the creatures had withdrawn and left them alone. While they were talking together, masses of people gathered outside the tent they were sitting in, and when they emerged from it, they were greeted with such cheering and cries of, "Hurray!" that it woke up the little prince in his crib. He cried at the noise and clamour, but after calming him down, Eythana brought prince Myrathion to see his father.

The moment Mojastic saw his little son again, was a touching one, and when he lifted him up and held him, the little infant studied his father intently with his now lilac-coloured eyes, and then he smiled. A sigh went through the crowd standing around them, and Mojastic lifted his face to the sky and closed his eyes, while the last bit of frost in his heart melted into tears of joy down his cheeks; he was home.

Many miles above the scene, a glowing orb floated lazily on the winds, gently bobbing. From the orb could be heard song and laughter. The song was a woman's, and the gentle laughter, a man's, both sounding very happy and content. Snuggling into Rajan's arms, Ahroree smiled up at his face and said, "Are you restless, my dear?"

"No," came the answer, "I am not restless, I am content. But I may become restless later, when we both start looking for something to do. What then?"

"There is no need for worry," she said, "the fates will call us when there is work to be done, and then we will have plenty to do! But for now, we have time to enjoy each other, and that is…"

"The hardest work of all!" he replied with a grin. Sailing into the sunset and on into the night, the orb continued with its gentle bobbing, floating over a sleeping world, dreaming in the starlight.

.